AYLA

M. P. Berger

ISBN-13: 9798698299240

Independently published

Edited by Jacqueline Hritz

Original Cover Art by: Fantasy & Coffee Design

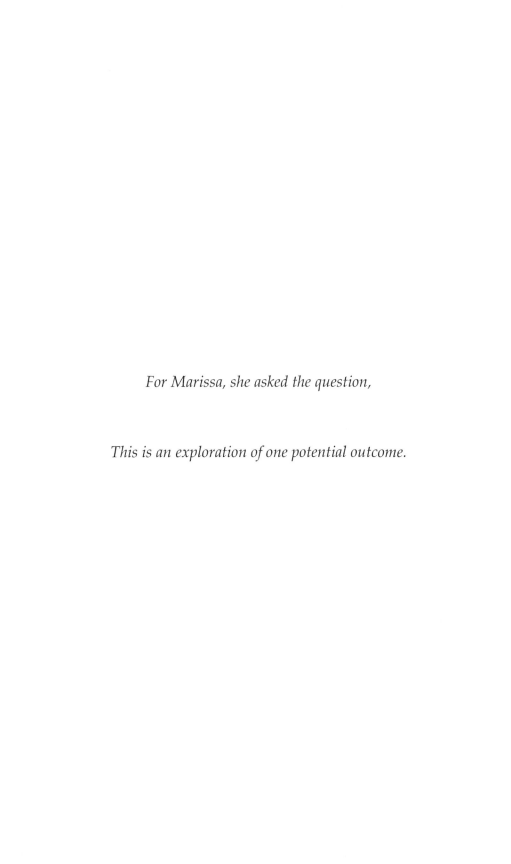

For Marissa, she asked the question,

This is an exploration of one potential outcome.

ONE

Life ends. It's a cold moment, unlike the glass Ivan's head rested against. With his eyes closed, he can picture himself at the beach; the warmth radiating is the sun, not the energy venting from the other room. The one he can no longer enter, where he can no longer be beside her. The bright lights still find their way to him; even in the darkness of closed eyes, he sees what they're doing to her, feels it.

He stares at his palm as the man in the nicely fitting suit and pulled-back hair says something with excited glee beside him. Ivan can still feel the cold. He's transfixed by it. His wife's once warm flesh, it changed. It was lost to the cold of the ending of a life. And here the man in the suit had been talking about the "Transitional Phase." Except, Ivan, he'd felt her leave, felt her move on.

Ivan's wife died. This was a fact, and Ivan accepted it with closed fists, with tears, with internal curses, with the feelings that her cold hand in his birthed.

And the guy in the suit—Chad, he'd call him—didn't seem to think this was a problem. "Amazing, isn't it?"

That wasn't the word choice that came to Ivan's mind when seeing his wife beyond the looking glass. A husk of her former self, a metal prod in the back of her skull, various tubes stuck to skin sucking who-knows-what from her. Her blank eyes staring at the ceiling as if it held the answers to the universe, in that state between the cracks of life and death.

Chad kept talking, didn't notice Ivan's shudder from a mere glance at what used to be his wife, "See those numbers and symbols flowing into our portable core? Those are strings of her consciousness, fragments that will be spooled and reconnected in what we call the 'mind plains.' It's magnificent to watch." Chad's unbridled excitement reminded Ivan of a boy, that's what he was, one dressed in adult clothes. Ivan wished he could sum up a fraction of what must be bubbling inside of Chad. Ivan longed for reverie in this moment, to find the warmth in the light of this place. All was bright, flashes and colors, but nothing penetrated him anymore.

"This is but a stopgap to an endless existence. You, no both of you, have made the right choice today." Ivan flinched at the touch on his shoulder. "Trust me."

Life ends, but there was a defiance to the natural order now. Still he saw the images flash before his mind, the cold, empty bed without his wife's weight depressing it. Their daughter's eyes transfixed on the bowl of cereal. A dusty chair in the study.

He didn't want to do this alone. He didn't want to do any of life's happenings without another. So he'd promised her. He bought the promise the ones in the suits proposed. It was done.

Life ends, or at least that's what Ivan had been taught. An outcome designated by the natural order of the universe. A final point, a moment to be marked in mind and memory, wrapped in a bow of meaning. Without such, everything becomes fuzzy, a shadow in the night, even if there's no way to distinguish the two.

Yet he'd promised. Ivan had to believe this was the right choice for her, for his daughter, and hopefully for him.

Ivan's hand wouldn't stop shaking from the cold, from death's lingering touch.

TWO

Seeing ones work in another's hands brought joy rather than the prick of lack of control. Their way of manipulating, the speed, what drew focus, it fascinates Ivan sometimes more than the actual process of creation. To be a bystander again in his own world.

"I'm impressed." Those words paired with Kendra's voice were not common. She waved the back of her hand across Ivan's workspace wall. His animation creation of floating splotches of yellow and red swirled together like they were liquid and not nature. Ivan loved this transition. The yellow rained down to become a field of sunflowers while the red shot to the sky, morphing into a red, glowing sphere that dripped its own fluids down onto the sprouting nature. Kendra paused the animation with a flick of her fingers. "Colors are brighter than your usual, I think you've gotten out of your rut." Ivan had plenty of ruts in his long, arduous career of fighting with his self-esteem and it tended to come out in his work first.

"I think it speaks to the fertility of new parents."

"Is that what this one was about? Clever. These are those wilderness advocates aren't they? A solid connection." Kendra smiled, another anomaly to her behavior. "People and their lust to have kids, no offense."

Ivan twirled his pen while he sat on the plush, carpeted floor, shoes off, picking at the fraying fabric of his lime-green socks. He gave a soft sigh. "I stopped at the one."

"Huh." Ivan wasn't sure if she directed it at his work, which was now in regular motion, dancing across his off-set studio space from the main hub of the office, or his comment about stopping at one child, because one was enough, and Kendra wouldn't know, never even had a pet. Three pen twirls later and Kendra had sped through the last portion of his work; she stopped twice to rewind, seeing the red sphere crack open and drip. His egg of time spilling out over the flowers and burying them. Only a few vigilant ones survived, brighter, stronger, and twice as big. A family outliving life, it's what it reminded Ivan of, what he made it become. "Huh."

"Am I missing something?"

"Not at all, it's beautiful and, what's the right word for, transient, or, no, smooth comes to mind. Simple and elegant, and just smooth. This is some of your best work in months. We're going to have some satisfied customers here. I'd like to catalogue this and put it in our annual showcase, a prime example of what we're striving for."

Boss lady was surprising Ivan more and more. She was beaming a smile back as she sent the project back to his work computer with a wave of her hand. She already had her CoMM out and was making a copy. A ping and a notification popped up on the monitor...Well, this was good, really good, for Ivan.

"Wonderful, glad to have you back among the stars. You can leave early if you want, see the one kid," she softly chuckled to herself as she opened the door to the rest of the office, "though I know you won't. Not one to ever leave early, are you?"

Apparently it was a rhetorical question, for she let the door shut and headed to the next studio to continue her round of check-ins. He took time off—it was always inside these walls was all—staring at the white blankness to try and wrestle with what others wanted him to show them or what his mind couldn't show himself. An artist trapped in his own mind at times. Couldn't have been that long…could it?

Ivan grasped his C7 CoMM, a slate of white that hummed to life once it felt his touch. "Ayla, when's the last time I took time off?"

Two green eyes, pinched together as if thinking, blinked to life on his device. "Strange question coming from you. It's been three years and two hundred and twelve days to be exact."

Stating it'd been a while was a bit of an understatement. A little slice for himself was long overdue. Plus, he had to show Kendra she was wrong for once, not that he wanted to, maybe only a smidgen. Nearly four years was far too long; he hadn't even taken off a day in his new decade. He popped in his earpiece and slid the C7 into his trouser pocket as it hummed to power. "What was the occasion?" The panel into his office slid open as he approached.

"There's no specific event written in your log. But I can pinpoint why."

"Of course you can," Ivan said.

"I sense potentially a hint of jealousy in your tone."

"Observant."

"Would you like to know, or are you going to pout all the way home? Oh, don't forget to tell Lisa that her haircut looks good."

"Lifesaver." He exchanged pleasantries with Lisa, who was doing her routine of drinking more coffee than was humanly possible even though it was barely noon. Peppy without the caffeine, most days it was too much to take in, but Ivan was good at relying on his artist awkwardness to get himself out of conversations. His mother reminded him of that often. He liked to think of himself as tactful. "So are you going to tell me," Ivan said as he launched down the stairs. "Shoot, also send Boss Lady a message that I'm taking the rest of the day off. Can you do that too?"

"I can multitask, unlike you," Ayla said.

"Walking and talking here."

"Should I be a little snarky since she gave you some flak for not taking time off?"

"Yes, please, but subtle." The sun greeted him through the giant glass wall that led out to the world. It was bright and inviting, a half a day off to himself.

"Of course," Ayla said. "And your last day off was for Ezra's sixteenth birthday."

The bioscan beeped, and the giant double doors parted open. The scan beeped another chime. The doors remained open. Ivan took slow steps out into the city. The sun couldn't warm him as he started to turn to the station. People buzzing more akin to insects than human.

In almost four years he hadn't taken time off for any of her other birthdays. Was that wrong of him? He wrestled with that in the throng of bystanders as soft music began to build in his ear. He smirked. "Funny, very melancholy of you."

"You seemed distracted by the information I gave you."

Ivan sighed. "Just realizing how quickly time flies."

"You know how absurd that saying sounds, right?"

"I've been on a plane; time changes when I fly. Bet it's even different on the other planets."

Ayla took in a breath, even if it was an absurd notion, and said, "I'm going to stop you right there; you don't want to debate me on this topic."

"I know; turn up the music, sounds fitting for my day off."

"I sense sarcasm this time."

"Correct."

Ivan didn't have a plan, that was clear the moment he arrived home. It was midday. Ezra would still be attached to her studies, and June had her craft club this afternoon. A slice of life for Ivan and Ivan only. He twiddled his thumbs in the kitchen. Stood and sipped water. Checked the plants outside the front stoop. Paged through the neighborhood leaflet on said stoop of what was planned for the month, which was an ambitious number of events and made him glad that June was more the chat-it-up-with-the-neighbors type. Ivan checked the updates of the world from his CoMM; doom and gloom with humor sprinkled in, nothing new.

He sat and waited for inspiration on what people did when they had time off. When there was no one around to fill the void. Chores, people did chores. Although lots of people left those to the Bots. Not Ivan. Bots and he didn't mix; plus, that's what a kid was for and what he was for when his work ideas started to scrunch into an unreadable blurry mess at his desk.

No one could organize his clutter but him. He eyed the storage compartment beside his dwelling with disdain. No wonder he never took time off; this was what he got himself into.

The storage container is an off-teal, no bigger than a shed, but he knew he'd thrown everything in there when they first moved out to the suburbs, set the lock, and never opened it again. It's packed with things he convinced himself to hang onto thinking he'd need them in a couple months, when in reality, it was better to pitch it.

"Good afternoon, Ivan," the storage compartment blinked to him as he waved upon approach. He thought the idea of a monitor on it was unnecessary with their home so close, but he did find himself smirking at the monotone greeting. He placed his palm on the side panel, cooler than skin, even out in the heat of the day. The horizontal door opened and rode back into the narrow space of his clutter. And it was *his*. June was one of those use-it-or-donate-it types that Ivan was jealous of, and his daughter Ezra kept stuffing her clutter on shelves and under the bed as if she were made to be an architect with her expertise in spatial awareness.

Piles of plastic boxes, some vacuum sealed, others with color-coordinated lids, a relic of a cardboard box somehow still looking better than shabby; it made the space feel more imaginative, a child's attempt at creating a city inside a dome.

It wasn't *as* disorganized as he remembered, not that he'd thought about this place for some time, least as long as it had been since he'd had a day off. "Ayla, play some motivational music for sorting this disaster."

"Affirmative, Captain."

"Nice one." Crescendoing melodies swarmed his ears while he did his best to sort the towers into smaller towers, which was making the space feel more like a battlefield with him playing the diplomat trying to calm tensions on both sides. What didn't help the situation was that, one, it'd been a long time since he was in here, and that paired with an "older-brain memory," as Ezra liked to say, made it hard to plan ahead on the organization. Two, he didn't have the foresight to either buy clear bins or put the labels in a constant location. Past Ivan was senile even before he got grays.

Two hours passed, and he'd sorted a small pile of objects he couldn't identify and sprawled them haphazardly outside the compartment's entrance—designated the "eradicate later" area. Next to that he'd created a-less-than-equal sorting of towers of bins on two sides, and he was currently in the midst of swapping and coordinating colors to each of those. A start to a job semi-well-done. Some spots looked like he'd done more damage, like his floor-to-ceiling tiered organizing shelf at the back of the space. It was somehow crooked and leaning at the same time from all the hectic moving about he'd been doing.

Should've gone with a wooden shelf. He kicked the bending plastic, and something slid off the top. It landed with the smallest rattle on a bin. A thin, black box, no thicker than half a finger, with a blue circle embossed on the top. Ivan stopped the music. He stopped everything from flooding in.

He pressed a thumb to the middle circle, and the single clasp holding the lid clicked. A pop, and the lid half opened and vented air. Teeth digging into bottom lip, Ivan flicked the box's lid back. Inside was a smaller white puck with a single blue outline on its surface. It hummed as his finger caressed the crevice of the outline.

What used to be his wife, contained inside this device, found once more, ready to be immortal. His promise to her shouting inside his mind over and over as his finger kept tracing the outline, as if the touch would bring it to life, as if it would bring her touch back to him. The weight of what he could do, what he hadn't been able to do, of what could be, knotting his stomach.

He owed her.

He owed his daughter.

Ivan abandoned his project and took his wife back inside the house with him.

THREE

Where Ivan wore his bright colors to and from work, Ezra left hers to populate the spaces she inhabited. It left her to wear only neutrals; today was an all-black kind of study day. Thankfully, she wasn't jacked into the system working on a project with classmates, and he was left to stand in awe of her chaotic organization of shelves lining every wall of her bedroom. An album of photos projected over the mass of objects cluttering the space. Souls captured in time looked jarring stretched over stuffed animals, glasses full of marbles, wooden sculptures, and well, Ivan couldn't identify half the memorabilia she collected from her game arenas.

Ezra was nose deep in her CoMM, her finger translating notes to the C-Slate mounted to the wall without taking eyes off the original device. Pride puckered Ivan's cheeks into a smile. Her innate ability to stay focused and motivated in spite of all the distractions was a rare treat to behold. She sure didn't inherit Dad's doldrum brain.

He took a seat on the edge of her bed. It was so low, it made his knees bend uncomfortably up to his chest, as if he were trying to cradle into himself. Kind of suited the moment. He reached over to his daughter's desk and set down his wife underneath her C-Slate.

Somehow she had the focus to finish the sentence she was on before popping out her earpiece. The room brightened to an eye-squinting white. The projector froze from its perpetual cycling. She swiveled to face her father, drumming a finger across her lower lip with eyes on her mother's puck, where her consciousness slept.

A wordless exchange of eyes on and off the device from the both of them. Until Ezra spoke two words: "Why now?"

Ivan saw her dormant pain. His stomach knotted as the images of Ezra staring into a cereal bowl came to mind, like they always did, with that empty chair beside her. "Honestly, forgot it was there." And that sounded much worse when it was out in the open. Like he'd forgotten that part of his life, about Ezra's mother, and he didn't want that to be it. Ivan wrapped his arms around his legs. "You know how long it took me to rebuild, to even come to terms with this. It doesn't mean I think anything less of her."

"I know, Dad." She hesitated halfway with a hand toward his. An awkward moment of it hanging out there, a half bridge that he could complete. Instead he tightened his hold, and her hand went to her mother and she traced the puck, the blue circle coming to life under the stroke of her finger. "Just, I feel like we've been here before, haven't we? You were so against it before."

"Against" was an improper word he thought; still, it might be what was coursing through him, even with his promise dragging a blanket of constant pricks across his legs. So convinced when he held it in his hand again that this was the time, and already he was doubting it all again. There was a simple explanation for the constant, revolving fulfillment of the idea of bringing her back; it was facing her, how to even begin to go about it. Face what was his wife, or what a fragment of her, had been or what they told him she would be—his wife, once more herself. It scared him into a continuous bout of self-doubt that was better corked and set aside, forgotten, locked away, and put out of sight.

All the money, all the time, its creation had cost, and still he had left it alone. Unused, like his wife was an object that didn't get to choose when to be awakened. Ivan had been selfish, and he deserved the hurt that built a nest inside his daughter's eyes. A constant reminder when the conversation about mother was revisited.

Ivan chose to talk to the device rather than Ezra. "This isn't me saying I'm ready; this is me approaching the subject with more distance." "Subject," come on Ivan—like she was one of his projects needing attention. Was it normal to be so disconnected from what had been, what his day-to-day had revolved around?

"Glad you're finally leveling up, ready to face the mid-boss at least."

"I vaguely have an idea of what you're implying."

"You're taking the first steps. Again. For your future, our future, it's going to be...weird isn't it?"

Ivan finally let his legs slack. "I think so."

Ezra's mouth formed a smirk as she swiveled to face her desk once more. She woke her C-Slate and gave Ivan a side-eye. "June is gonna be fucking pissed."

It could get complicated. "Maybe, and hey, don't use that language."

"Pissed isn't even that bad; everyone in the sessions says it, even Ms. Sally." Ivan pulls out the dad stare from his repertoire, which is nothing more than scrunching his eyebrows and putting thumb under chin. Ezra counters with her aloof-teenager shrug, which only makes the dad stare more potent. "Seriously, though, Dad. You think she's going to be ok with this? Think, Mom, will be ok with, you know?"

"Lots of variables," Ivan put his hands to his face. "Don't even know where to begin to navigate this one."

"It's going to be hard to guess how she's going to react. A true RNG catastrophe." Ivan scrunched his brow; there were too many phrases to keep up with. "RNG—random number generator. Come on, Dad, that one's easy. Unlike what you have to decide, because, you know." Ezra's tone dropped an octave, and she pushed out the end of her sentence with a sigh. "It's always up to you."

Ivan left the room with his hand shaking from an unfelt breeze.

FOUR

June is a razor blade of beauty, composed of sharp and sleek edges. Deep cuts no matter which way Ivan found himself looking at her, even now, "beautiful" shouldn't be the first descriptor applied to someone washing dishes. Yet it was there, invading Ivan's brain and spilling out of his mouth. "God, you're beautiful." He meant it with every fiber of his being.

June's response was that smile that lit up Ivan's insides to a dance. It was also paired with the shaking of her head, the usual dismissive response to the "far too many compliments" Ivan gives—her words, not his. Crumbles of dessert long abandoned sat on the kitchen island between them. Daughter holed up in her room jacked in or back to studying like the rigorous machine she'd become. Ivan, left with the calming mundane, wide patches of serenity. June had her ambient country noises filling the kitchen, and the translucent counters danced with images of meadows moving from a synthetic gentle breeze. The opaqueness of the ceiling turned down to watch the setting sun and the welcome intrusion of dotting stars. Ivan never tired of these moments. Except, he had his wife in his pocket. He pressed the outer case with a finger to remind himself of the absurdity of this, of the mar he could put on what his life had become.

Ezra had given him looks all throughout dinner - yes, they still sat around the dinner table, three beings in the same room no matter how much the world evolved—her eyes trying to pry out the beginnings of the conversation from him. He'd told her, but somehow couldn't tell June. Where the disconnect was eluded Ivan then, and a bit now as he reveled the simplicity of watching another go about a chore, another chore that could be done by a Bot or fancy machine, but June had also leaned in to the belief that doing something yourself gave a bit of pride.

Washing dishes bringing pride, one would think they were crazy to have such feelings, and maybe eight of ten times, they would be correct. Ivan only wished he knew the ratio of good to bad in telling June about awakening his wife. That's not to say he hadn't mentioned her, told tales about her, had her photos up, but this was a bit different, more life-altering.

The surprise he felt when finding her in the storage compartment among his other discarded and kept-safe things. He'd forgotten, not moved on; there was a difference. He wrestled as much with that as with the impulse to slap the puck on the island and be done with this. Make the decision cut and clean, this was what he had to show, and they could talk. That's all he wanted. He didn't even know if he was ready.

Ivan didn't know if he was ready.

How could he bring June into the fold? He stood from the island, shame pricking at his heels as he walked away from her with his wife clutched in pocket. He escaped into their room and set the device inside his bedside drawer with the rest of the supplies that he thought he'd need in the middle of the night and never did. There might be some ironic theory on that, but again, it eluded Ivan, like these tough conversations always tended to.

He tidied up the drawer, what would now be his wife's new place of residence until he summoned the courage to face what he actually wanted to do with his wife. No, his dead wife, she died back then; he let her go, or at least, he thought he did. Except he'd kept her, he'd paid for her to be preserved, brought her all the way out to the suburbs to be in his new life. He closed the drawer. Not tonight. There was distance enough, he thought, he believed, he knew but couldn't form it into words yet.

FIVE

He hears her. The subtle sweetness of her voice, a hummingbird of noises flapping around Ivan's mind. Her voice distant in the blackness of the void. Idle chatter he couldn't pinpoint; it all became washed-out gibberish. Still, he knew it was her in that dark place. Warmth, even in the cold darkness.

He couldn't remember the last time he'd dreamed, and he wanted nothing more than to stay in that special place of darkness and her. Wishing and wanting, he had a semblance of control to direct the dream. He took the initiative to will himself to hear the words. If he were to stay, he wanted to know what she was muttering about. He stretched out his arm in that void and felt a soft nothing.

His eyes were open. The curtains drawn, the minimal yellow glow of his display clock—the fluorescent relic that June still made fun of him from time to time—and sleep sticking to his body from the confines of a warm bed. Confusion wrapped tighter than the sheets.

Her voice, her voice was still talking, muffled, farther away, like a dream he hadn't been dreaming. He was awake.

Ivan's hand felt the empty space beside him—June wasn't there. The digital display shot yellow illumination as his feet touched an already-warm floor. He worked sleep from his eyes and let his ears take in the sounds. Two people muttering beyond his bedroom door. Still unable to discern what they were saying, he recognized the pitches of both of his wives. Thinking that made this feel more dream-like than anything else as Ivan dressed with haste rather than taste.

Hesitation clamped his hand shut on the doorknob. Open it, go out there, and meet them with a head held high. Ivan, you've done enough worrying for more than one lifetime.

Ivan wasn't ready last night; what could a bit of sleep change? Not that he had a choice, she was out there, he knew it, could hear her; this wasn't a dream, and if it was, his mind deserved an award, for this was a damn good creation. *Get on with it, it's your wife, don't be scared of that*, Ivan pumped that mantra throughout his mind enough times for his body to be ready to take on the challenge.

Deep breath and Ivan swung open the door.

White lights were set to a soft dim. The whispers, that's why he couldn't understand them, immediately stopped at the sound of his approach. He hadn't even looked at the time; it felt early, even though he couldn't describe why—that was an oddity he would revisit later if he found time, a good project idea. The ceiling was set to full opaque as he found himself standing in the kitchen. June was hunched over the landing with a cup filled with something steaming, her bedtime gown still hugging her skin.

Beside his wife was his wife.

An almost perfect recreation, minus a new hazy tint of blue surrounding her skin as if the aura of her soul were coming to life. It was her, a few years younger than when he'd last seen her living—that's what stood out to him most acutely—but it was his wife. Standing in his kitchen beside June, as if she had never left him. As if the cancer never took her too soon.

There was no stopping him. He bolted to her side and shot

out his hands. He wrapped his hands around his wife only to hug air and topple into the fridge. There was a gasp, his breath leaving, maybe someone else's too. He sat there, collecting himself, forehead against the fridge, a cool spot as warmth ran down his cheeks. "I'm sorry." Ivan pressed his palms into the fridge, stabilized, and got back on his feet. He wiped at his eyes, and again, he said the words, "I'm so sorry. I just, I don't know."

"Don't be, I had the same compulsion, even if we can't." His wife put a hand to her face as if she could actually touch her own skin. "Oh my, it's really you."

It was her. It was truly her. Ivan cracked a smile. "Think that's supposed to be my line."

She laughed—how he'd missed that sound. The rise and fall of her breaths forced out in small bursts. The way her nose crinkled with its own furrow lines, as if it were concentrating on not laughing and failing miserably. With that singular sound, paired with her face, all the worries of what to do, how to act, what was right and wrong in the face of her once again, were blown away. Cares no longer existed; it was his wife, and that was enough. He'd been an imbecile for being worried and scared of this moment when it was such a beautiful and, daresay, transcendent moment in his life.

Ivan's wife, standing before him, looked over her own hands as if she too had to take a moment and remember what she was and what she'd been doing before Ivan walked into the kitchen. Her head jerked to June. A quick bow. "I'm so sorry, that was so rude of us."

June pointed with a firm finger, "Don't even start with the apologies again. This is new for all of us. Besides, I would have reacted the same. Maybe there would have been even more crying involved if roles were reversed." Ivan raised an eyebrow at that; he couldn't use two hands with the times he'd seen his wife cry—well, his newer wife. "We didn't wake you, did we? We were doing our best to stay hushed."

"Do you still drink coffee when you wake up earlier than scheduled?" His old wife asked.

"He does. A rarity to see him up twenty minutes before he has to rush out of here to get on the tram." June sent a sly look over to Ivan as she started up the brew.

"Some things haven't changed; that's good to hear."

His wives exchanged short bursts of laughter. The back of Ivan's head was cool from the fridge; his tears were dried, but his mind was spinning. It couldn't be this simple. She was back and everything…clicked. They were getting along so easily.

Should it be this easy? Ivan thought not, and yet his heart was no longer hammering in his chest as he listened to their conversation. A bystander, even though he was the topic of their constant stream of comments and questions.

Life had changed, and somehow it was adapting at a rate he couldn't even process. She was here like she'd never left, and he didn't want her to leave ever again if this was how it was going to be. How could he have been scared before?

"Honey?" Lost in thought, he wasn't even sure which of them had said it. He extended his hand and took the coffee offered to him. "You all right?" June asked more with body than words.

His wife—both "old" and "new," one could say—crept a few paces closer. "This must be stimuli overload. Sorry, love." She gave a half glance to June, but she was inspecting Ivan as if he were a specimen who'd awoken in an unfamiliar world and was about to bolt. It was an on-point assumption.

Ivan took another sip of coffee and set the steamy mug on the island, raised his hands, and slipped between the two without a backwards glance. A bit ridiculous, knowing he could go through one of his wives without any resistance; that would be hard to get used to. "Need a shower" was all that came out as he ducked inside his room. He closed the door and gave out the biggest sigh he could muster. This was going to take a little bit of getting used to.

He stripped off his clothes, balled them up, and tried his best to make it in his laundry bin with no success; nothing changed there. He studied his array of colors, all of them drawing his attention at once, saying *pick me*, when there was only enough of him to go around for one.

Ivan wasn't really thinking about clothes, suffice it to say.

"You've lost the baby chub." Ivan slammed his sock drawer closed and backed up into his closet, covering his genitals. "I miss it, but you look great, sweetums." His wife had manifested on the side of his bed, a glint of light coming off his lamp as if she'd once been connected to it by some ethereal process he couldn't comprehend.

Ivan took a random shirt from his closet and put it around his waist. "Thanks. June, she's got me on a routine." His wife tilted her head at that, a small smirk forming. "I feel fantastic. Miss some of the cheats, still get them, bit more reserved, I'd say."

"What're you doing?"

"Getting ready to shower, like I said." Ivan followed her eyes to what his shirt was covering. "Oh, well, don't know, really."

His wife came to be beside him. "It's been so long since I've seen you, and you're not letting me see the goods? How cruel of you, husband." The play in her voice, the way she sauntered, her shoulders and hips in unison, it was her doing what she did best, getting Ivan focused on her. "You've done well for yourself—your health, June, this place. I'm glad. But please, don't be distant with me. I've been waiting for this."

A slash of hurt played over her face as Ivan took a step away. "June will wonder where you are. Best for us to talk in the open, I think. Well, I don't know, but it sounds like that would be best; no secrets that way."

"Oh, Ivan, you are so sweet and so aloof. But sure, I'll get back to your wife. You shower and take the time you need. We'll all sit down and chat again soon."

His new/old wife vanished from his bedroom. He wasn't sure if the voices of his wives had always been there or if they'd just gotten louder out in the kitchen, but they were there, buzzing inside his ears, growing into a hive, that could only be drowned out by the rush of scalding water cascading down his skin, making a cocoon for him to think and take it all in.

SIX

Pockets of clustered neighborhoods, the taste of burnt coffee on tongue, and chirping of birds in the ears, the spaces close enough to know pleasantries and vast enough to slip out without notice or care. A dichotomy of ideals that battled with one another, privacy of home interconnected with a community that wanted to gather and yet wanted to be addressed as separate entities. Distinction between the two determined by a list of variables—current news, weather, what happens behind closed doors, and what happens in the communal spaces, to make the list short. Judgements made based on individuals following protocol and by overstepping normalcy.

The desolate quiet when children had been lured into their homes by hot meals—the few that still knew what "go outside and imagine" meant—had grown on Ivan. The waning moment, he coined it with dual meaning, for its duration was minuscule and the opportunities to witness it drifted as the years of projects consumed him, turning into weeks rather than days between exposures. Time changed, or Ivan changed within it and emerged having learned to not miss the bustle of the city. Long nights that one took. Sleeping through the night was its own chore before the cancer. After, the noises wormed their way inside; then he couldn't shut off his head in the silence of the suburbs. Too long did he wander in the spaces between fits of sleep and revolutions of anxiety before the quiet soothed the noise in his head as opposed to stirring it.

The quiet and Ivan got along most days now. The pesky neighbors and the overly pleasant ones were tolerated to a most gracious degree. The further walk to the station hub was motivation to keep up routines rather than a deterrent from a lackluster hobby of sleeping in. Ivan had changed little, and yet he felt like a different person sometimes when he found himself smiling as he passed a park, the one local cafe, the bar that was too far away. How malleable the will of a man can be when another's influence shows an alternate viewpoint. June loved the suburbs. Ivan did not. June pointed out the perks, and Ivan listed the determents. He'd transformed into another Ivan—lost to talks about walking hiking trails and having enough space to fit a new lover's crafts, a daughter's growing shelves, and a father's insistence on hoarding memories in a variety of fashions.

Ivan learned to love again in more ways than one, and it would seem he'd be doing something vaguely familiar once more.

The doors to the station hub were propped open by a steady stream of people with heads down or yapping to invisible people, or at least Ivan, liked to think that or pretend there was someone beside them, and he'd daydream about what they would look like floating over each person like a speech bubble from the comic days.

Ivan activated his C7 and held it out in front of him. A silent ping swept out from his CoMM, that only the slightest vibration could be felt in his fingertips. A representation of the quickest route to his tram digitized on the walkways of the station. The train's scheduled departure counted down at the top of his display; he'd be in there earlier than normal for a change.

"Shall I prepare for your commute, Ivan, the usual jazz tunes?" Ayla's voice chimed in from his earpiece.

"Sounds like perfection." He saw his own caricature from a bystander's point of view in his mind's eye. He wondered what avatar they concocted for him to be talking to.

"It will be done." Ayla's voice took in a breath as if she needed oxygen. "Did I get the voice right this time?"

Ivan was letting her work on interrogating that alien voice from a relic computer game to her speech patterns. "You're getting darn close. Don't know why Ezra loves something from heaps of decades, before she was even a thought in our minds, so much."

"I could simulate the code; there are still copies of Starc—"

"No need. I like you trying to replicate, more fun that way."

"As you say. Would you like me to read your messages before your musical escape, Ivan?"

"Sure thing, Ay-Ayla." The name stuck on his tongue. It was burnt coffee without the satisfying gulp of something energizing finding its way down the throat. Tasteless suburbs shouldn't ever be a thing.

"Ezra says—"

"Wait. Is it possible to change the name I've given you?" He waved his CoMM over one of the many doors of the train, and it opened. The lights on the ground showed him which seat was preferable for his time allotment until his exiting stop.

"Do you not like my name anymore?" She sounded offended.

"No, I do." Of course he did. He loved the way the name sounded. "Looking for a change is all."

"What would you like?"

"I don't know. How about you pick?"

"Me?" There was a pause. "Are you sure, Ivan?"

"Yes, I give you authority to choose your own name." He settled into his seat where the temperature on the handles was already beginning to cool to his liking.

"Such a daunting task, but I've picked."

"That was quick."

"I work with haste when required to." Ivan let out a chuckle at her mix of self-flattery and matter-of-fact tone. "Holiday."

"Ah, clever girl."

"I thought you'd appreciate my choice. I'll also respond to Holi for short, if that's to your liking."

"Yes, permission granted."

"Would you like me to continue, or more like "start," reading your messages?"

"Ya know, turn up the jazz, and I'll enjoy losing myself to it."

"It will be done."

SEVEN

The morning had slipped away from Ivan, with the confusion of two wives and a new project. New work always came in with the best of timing; this project from a favorite client of Ivan's, so he'd set aside half the morning for working out a basic concept. Sketches were littered across the image tiles on his wall, and he kept flipping and messing with the timeline for which one would come first. He already had the first major transition sorted out, but there was so much left to do. Lost in work, he'd forgotten how his daughter would react to, you know, having her mother again. Again, that sounded rather bad inside Ivan's head.

"Holiday, pull up my messages please, priority from family."

"As you say." Ivan's monitor mirrored the display of his C7. Ezra's name bolded.

Right, time to dig in.

Ezra: So…June uploaded Mother, glad I'm not a gambling girl. Fucking wild morning, total random encounter, thanks for that.

Dad: Shit. It's been a whirlwind of a day. Should have sent a message while I headed to work—

Now Ivan felt guilty for taking the solace time with music and not checking his messages. Like she'd said, at least he could have given her a warning of some kind. The turmoil he put himself through that morning, wondering if it was still a dream —he could have at least saved her from that.

Dad: —forgive me, it's been a strange morning.

Ezra: No language police today, you're having a go of it.

TimeReal?

Ivan glanced at the fluorescent display on his desk—yes, he had a relic at work too—he'd still have plenty of time for check-ins afterward. "Holiday, secure the room please."

"My path is set." She was sticking with the video game voices this week. His studio locked, lights dimmed, and the glass frosted.

"Thank you, Holiday." Ivan opened TimeReal on his C7 and gestured from the device to the floor of his studio. A green disk digitized on the floor. He kicked up his feet on the desk and leaned back in his chair.

Dad: Ready when you are

A ping vibrated his CoMM, and he accepted Ezra's TimeReal. The green disk blinked and generated a cylinder of green light where Ezra's projection manifested. "Hey, little love."

"Hold on, your feet are cut off." Her manifestation showed her dragging her fingers across her CoMM. "There we go. Hey back."

"Needed to see my feet that bad, huh?"

"Not all of us can lounge while working or studying." She sat on the edge of her bed with a smirk. "Totally kidding. Working on anything fun?"

"Actually, yeah. It's been a good week. Finalizing a project and starting a new one. I love the beginning stages, even if my head is all over the place."

"But the work makes it easier to focus."

Ivan clicked his tongue. "I've probably said that handful of times before, haven't I?"

"More like dozens. Least you can block out the weird, I can't."

"It's a skill." His wife's deathbed shot to the forefront of his mind. There he was, holding her cold hand. Those images stayed, but the nights he couldn't sleep; those images never surfaced, it was the lack of weight on the other side of the bed that kept him up, not the circumstances of being alone. "Whether that's a good thing is still up for debate. So, how are you taking…all this."

Ezra cradled her chin in her hands. "It's everything I wished for back then. And somehow, I don't know how to be…or act in general. It's so weird."

Ivan was nodding along with each of her statements trying to not think about how he'd failed Ezra's wants to protect his own. "I know. I tried to hug her right away, stupid I know."

"We're both dumb. I tried to do the same."

Ivan unbuttoned his collar. "Looks like you're still my daughter. Hey, I'm sorry I didn't tell you. That was a major dad mess-up."

"I know, I know. Honestly, I'm more surprised that June is so…" Ezra furrowed her brow. "Wow, I can't think of a good word for it."

"Complacent."

"Good one. Yeah, like, seriously, you should hear those two; they are being all giddy with one another like schoolgirls."

"Going to take some getting used to."

"On your end even way more so, like who do you go to bed with? Both? Do you rotate?" Ivan bit his lower lip. This was a weird conversation to be having with his daughter, even if she was an adult. "I can tell this is making you uncomfortable. I mean I suppose it's natural for a man to love more than one woman, or vice versa. Happens a lot actually."

"Bit different, this."

"Totes."

"No one says that anymore, kiddo."

"I've entered the deep realms; we're a rare breed, but we exist."

"There you go, back to being your mom's kid. Always thought I was the strange one."

"You are." She took her CoMM and tapped out a message. There were too many connections in her life for Ivan to begin to fathom who it was. Another blessing—she didn't get more of dad's reclusiveness. "Got to go, Daddio. Study session calls."

"Be careful."

"I won't overwork my brain, don't worry."

Ivan wasn't implying that, and he shouldn't even be thinking about that sort of thing. But again, he had a creative mind that liked to twist what a study session looked like from his time to her time. Things changed or people actually did study from time to time. "Love you. See you tonight."

"Love you too."

The green disk faded, and the quiet of his studio returned. Ivan spun and stretched his arms, with a series of pops coming from his shoulders. "Holiday, any appointments today?"

"None." There was a subtle vibration on the desk from his CoMM. "There is a calendar event, though not in your itineraries like your usual methods."

Bit odd, that. "What's on the calendar?"

"Firmware Proactive Home Security Hub Update."

Ivan grabbed his CoMM and found the calendar. There was indeed an event added. He clicked on it; it wasn't for another hour or so. Normal, minus the fact that he hadn't added it.

Perhaps June did. That would make sense with all their sharing. He should send her a message, heck, no, he should call. Not because he was paranoid, obviously not; because he needed to check in on her as much as his daughter. Even if Ezra seemed to think his wives were getting along swimmingly. June and his wife at home alone; that was not something he thought he'd ever say.

"Holiday, prep full display."

"Initiating."

Ivan's monitor widened, and the camera light blipped into existence. He clicked on June's profile. She answered on the second round of signals. "Well, this is unexpected. How's it going?" There was only blackness displayed on her end, minus her avatar photo.

"Afternoon, love. Things are good, surprisingly. New project came in today, been putting my head down and starting the process."

"You do love beginnings don't you?" Ivan needed to stop repeating the same old lines. "I like that shirt on you, by the way. Makes your eyes stand out."

"Thanks."

"You rarely call. You want to talk to Ayla?"

"No, I mean, yes, of course." He stumbled over his thoughts. Was it right to want to be talking to his old wife instead of his current? "But no, I was only checking in; that's all."

"Oh, ok. Well things are going swell. Ayla is wonderfully analytical, which is a welcome change. I can finally relate to someone in the household; Ezra has her moments. Oh, did you catch her before you left?"

"No, but I touched base before I called. She seconds you and Ayla getting along by the way. Bit surprised." Ayla's face, looking like it did on her deathbed, filled his monitor for a single blink.

Ivan pinched and minimized the feed into a smaller section. He played the static avatar in rewind. No other image popped up.

"What's wrong?"

"Nothing. Seeing things, I think. Oh, there was one thing, popped into my head just now."

"Sure it did."

"Hey, now," Ivan pulled up his CoMM and tapped on his calendar. "Did you happen to add a shared event on the—" It was gone. Ivan clicked on the date, and there weren't any new events.

"Honey, you all right?"

Ivan knew he was taking too long to respond. His eyes, transfixed on his display. It vanished. He made a show of it, rubbed his eyes, and did another stretch. "Must be a bit tired and disoriented. Not enough coffee, I guess, or maybe it's doing the opposite since it's been a while. It's been a different kind of morning."

The black screen dissipated, and June was there standing beside the door, the camera awkwardly looking up her nose. She looked down into the camera. "I'm sorry about that. I know it has to be a lot to take in at once."

"Just a bit, I was—" Ivan was warming up to the idea of awakening his own wife, to opening the floodgate once again and living with hope, even if he'd moved on; or at least, he thought he had. But that's not something he could say if Ayla were there listening—letting her know he hadn't made up his mind. "I was caught off guard is all."

"Not the greatest surprise, I know. You've told me stories for so long, why waste this opportunity, so I figure jump in and get it over with, right?"

"That's one way to do it."

"You're not mad?"

"Of course not." Only a little that such an important choice was taken from him, that the time to prepare was lost, and now he had to stumble through it or sink in its waves.

"Good, now I gotta go, love. I have to make a store run for some ingredients."

"Now you are making this day truly strange. You're cooking?"

"Ayla is going to coach me; apparently you love meatloaf and never cared to share that little tidbit."

It was because he'd tried many others, and nothing could compare. In some people's lives there's a realization that life wouldn't get any better than it was in a certain moment, and they have to accept it, rather than chase the dream. Ivan and meatloaf, it was a done deal. He'd had the best, and he could accept that. "Sounds like it should be interesting. I can stop on my way home if you'd like?"

"Your lack of confidence is appalling. No need, you focus on you; let the morning surprise settle and give yourself time to adjust to this new situation we find ourselves in. I've got you tonight." She winked and blew Ivan a kiss before the display cut off.

That was the woman he loved. The one who understood his needs and the flow of Ivan's world. Or, at least, one of the women in his life who got him. This was going to take some getting used to.

EIGHT

A free afternoon before dinner, and he didn't even have to rush out of work to make it to the station on time. It was nice not being shouted at by the security Bot for running too fast on the bridge-ways. Even if the Bot's threat of being shocked hadn't come to fruition and he was a repeat offender.

The sun was warm, the bench warmer, and the traffic of people left him with enough entertainment as he waited for, well, nothing outside the Hub. There was delight in not needing to be anywhere, even if it was in a limited timeframe—freedom from the shackles of responsibility. He'd even silenced his CoMM and took the extra step to turn off the vibrations. Slow jazz and imagining the companions people talked to through their devices ticked away the time with lethargic grace.

It'd only been seven minutes.

How did people actually take the time and smell the flowers without going mad? Two days in a row of having time to spend on himself was throwing him for a loop. He should have stayed at work and ironed out a few more details, maybe made small talk with some of the other artists or even the data over-viewers.

He cleared notifications of updates; he had enough on his own plate instead of worrying about the people around him who liked to share the most mundane findings and thought it was profound. He spun his CoMM around, twirled it in one hand and then the other. A worn device, outdated by five months, soon to be the beginnings of something he should replace, was pushed to upgrade via personal notifications and deals, but he liked the weight of this one more than the ones before.

His device.

That gave him an option for killing time. "Holiday, set a course for OrionCircle's closest installation. I've got some questions."

NINE

OrionCircle was not subtle with branding. The entire installation right off Holiday's plotted stop was only two variations of colors: blue, white, and the rest transparent. A dome that had its opaqueness set to zero, so from a quick glance, the hexagons linked together as its framework could be written off as a stutter in the vision. The pathways, blue carpet —Ivan wished they felt like the real deal, they didn't—with the edges lined in white, like a one-way arrow into the central dome, which reminded Ivan of an oversized hollowed-out golf ball. "Oversized" didn't paint a proper picture; the sphere was nearly an entire city block—an old one, not the new developments where space became crucial. It was lined with personal kiosk stations where people were jacked into a reality of their choosing, a construct to give away the pleasures of travel with a home near you, or something like that. It was their big venture until OrionCircle's newest creation happened— DRIP, the procedure that made Ayla what she was today.

Ivan crossed the threshold, where the blue carpet ceased, and a manufactured warm breeze tickled his cheeks. He wasn't four steps in when he was greeted by a young woman whose face was far too excited at the revelation of Ivan walking into her domain. "Welcome to your new reality, good sir. May I interest you in a sampling of our new devices? It will only take a moment of your time, and then you'll be up-to-date on everything that can alter your reality today." She was already holding a C-Slate with an attached projection disk.

Ivan came to waste time and, well, get to the bottom of his finicky device. He shrugged his shoulders, "Sure."

"Excellent choice, excellent choice," a blue hologram with different spheres blipped above the slate. "A bevy of upgrades and cosmetic updates have been added, but I'll make sure to only include the newest designs since last time you were with us." A white light flashed, and Ivan could see his identification card pop up in the display. "You're long overdue, Ivan. Can we be on a first name basis? I feel like we can."

Another shrug. "Sure."

"Most excellent, most excellent. Now, we would be here much longer than individual permissions are allowed, so I'll make sure to give you the extraordinary highlights in case you haven't been keeping up with our feed." He sure hadn't, and by the undertone in Ms. Cheery's overwhelmingly pleasant voice, she knew that, too, based on whatever stats were displaying in her Retina Ring. "Firstly," she tapped on a sphere and it cracked open like an egg, Ivan found himself drawn to that transition, "the Chrono Line. It's our software upgrade for Home Cores to easily shift permutations of theoretical timelines into a best-suited plan for what you should be doing with your time off." Ivan and time off didn't get along. He also didn't like things deciding for him; Holiday at least weighed options most of the time. "It can also be paired with the navigation system of your CoMM, which I see you use fairly often. Could be a nice fit." Ivan raised an eyebrow, but Ms. Cheery was already swiping to the next product.

"Ah, yes, the OmniRing. Fully functional pairing of a DRIP with another suitable vessel." Ivan had just activated his wife;

well, not even him, but he wasn't about to dive into that one. He shook his head.

"Right, another item of intrigue, our photorealistic security camera makeovers. You've been keeping up with these, right? They are all over the feeds, the SC5s. They are reworking how we think of augmented realities." Ivan scratched at his chin. "You have some of the SC3s installed at your studio. Were you unaware?"

"Must have forgotten." Ivan knew there were cameras, but the specifics never intrigued him. It'd be so much easier if he cut to why he came, but he was a bit too nice to interrupt.

"Right, right, well then, I guess we'll move along then. AgeRefiner is a timely one for sure." Ivan did another eyebrow raise. "I'll give you the sales pitch. Tired of clipping grays? All you do is apply this thin mask, and you'll never need to do it again. Doesn't even feel synthetic. I can attest to the wonders of this one."

Ms. Cheery didn't look a day older than someone who hadn't finished her studies, what did she know about any sort of refinement? "Odd."

"You'd be surprised how many customers we get who want a little patchwork done." How OrionCircle branched off into the beauty department was something Ivan wasn't going to take the time to indulge himself with.

Instead of taking the bait on this one, Ivan gave an awkward half smile and shrugged. "Guess I'm alright with my patches and all."

There was not even a pause in a response. "The big question is, though, how can I help you, right now, today, with you being privy to all we have to offer?"

Splendid, he was out of what was beginning to feel like an interrogation rather than a listing. "I've got some kinda bug going on with my C7. Think it's interfering with my monitor at work and, well, seems to be a bit glitchy."

"C7, those shouldn't have any troubles, or, well, rarely at least. Refresh rates are about the only troubles, should look into getting a C7 3rd."

"Only looking to talk to someone about syncing disruptions is all."

"You know, I bet having us take a look at your CoMM more closely will help us narrow down any anomalies occurring. Kiosk eight is," a few taps on her C-Slate, "is prepped and ready for your arrival."

All that talk and he wasn't even going to get the help from a human. "Thanks."

"Find me if you have any troubles, but it's basic, you'll have it done in no time."

Ivan wasn't sure if the woman was oblivious to her condescending tone or if it had become ingrained after talking to tech-inept individuals like Ivan all day.

The kiosk was two tall, thin sheets of white plastic that gave a meager sense of privacy as he stepped up to it. A display appeared that filled the space between the edges of his kiosk. It showed a face that had no identifiable gender, only the eyes looking into Ivan, and somehow, he could tell they were smiling. A pleasant feeling.

The display opened inward below the eyes and a Bot hovered out, one designed to look like a hand-sized ladybug, except the colors were different, and if one were to guess white and blue, they would be correct, to no one's surprise. "Assistance required?"

Ivan held out his C7. "Yes, a scan for synching troubles, specifically between this device and linked software from home and work devices."

"Affirmative." The eyeballs blinked white a handful of times, seven to be exact; Ivan liked to count things when he was bored.

Every time the action occurred, it made a noise as if someone decided eyes blinking was akin to peeling a banana. OrionCircle sometimes made strange design choices to make their devices stand out from the competitors. "CoMM C7 is fully functional."

"I have my doubts."

"Would you like another scan?"

"Sure."

Ivan could guess the confirmation before it left the Bot's mechanical mouth. "Still fully functional." The bit of attitude, he didn't predict.

"Can I set up a manual scan?"

Another portion of the display opened inward, and a raised tray with a foam fitted layer to the exact dimensions of Ivan's CoMM jutted out. Ivan set his device inside. "Holiday, run diagnostics using external power."

"Commencing." The C7 illuminated white for a blink. "Complete. I am also seeing nothing out of the ordinary, which, to me, is quite troubling."

At least someone was on his side. "Ok, Bot, let me talk to a real person or send a ping to that…person…whoever helped me earlier."

The Bot stayed floating where it was until a panel in one of the privacy sides slid open and revealed a protruding C-Slate, sleeker than the everyday design. There was a lot of text. He gestured most of it away until he found the "Do you need further assistance?" option. He pressed it and verbalized "yes."

A blue light turned on at the top of the kiosk. A cone of light shot down, and an older man, with hard furrow lines under eyes and across his forehead, manifested beside Ivan with a familiar blue aura around him. Same as his wife. Another person, who came out on the other side of the Transitional Phase and lived on, a DRIP.

Close enough to a real person.

That thought made Ivan's tongue hesitate in the face of this new man. No, this person was as real as his old/new wife. Get that line of thinking out of your head, Ivan. "Hi."

"Hello."

Ivan took his C7 from the manual scanner as he fidgeted with his collar. Guess this man wasn't privy to what he wanted done. "So, these scans haven't been working, I've noticed a synching problem or a glitch, and so has Holiday, my System Interconnected Manager. Maybe this kiosk and that Bot haven't been updated."

The ladybug made a low clicking sound, no doubt directed at

Ivan. Stupid Bot.

The DRIP manifestation held out a finger and dabbed the CoMM as if he could actually feel it. Somehow Ivan felt a vibration run through his palm. "Your communication device has a trace of data that is linked to your home address. A double looping feedback error has occurred. It shouldn't happen again. I've contacted an associate to make sure you're satisfied with the process."

"I didn't ask—"

Ms. Cheery was at his side before he could debate another point. "Ivan, my good sir. Seems we've solved your troubles today. Took a bit more teamwork than I initially would have guessed. Sorry about that lack of foresight; that's on my end."

She was smiling; the DRIP wasn't, and Ivan was siding with DRIP. "Well, I don't, well, I'm a bit confused, this AI—"

"We don't use those terms around here." The smile broke, and there was a hard line for a moment or two. Then she was back, a bit more ghoulish to Ivan. "Please refer to Peter as what he is, a Digitized Representation Intellect of Person, DRIP. Quite easy. It's more accurate. Heck, call him by his first name; I find that to be the best approach."

Ivan wasn't sure if accuracy and representation went hand in hand. He made representations of people's stories, poems, fantasies, and they weren't the same thing because they didn't come from the original creator. Ivan had the freedom to interpret; he wasn't sure if Peter here had those shackles unlocked. "Sorry Peter, I was—"

"No offense taken, Ivan. Not everyone is used to me as a being. It takes some getting used to. Like any new device, even if I'm more sophisticated than all the devices you've ever held."

Couldn't override pompous in the Transitional Phase, it seemed. Strange that Peter here also thought of himself as a device versus a person; the divergence was troubling. "Haven't held you."

"Touché." That got the faintest twitch of a lip.

"Anyways, Peter here," Ivan turned back to the associate, "identified a problem with my C7, and he fixed it immediately."

"Sounds like a wonderful tale."

"He didn't ask."

"May inquire what you mean, sir?"

"For my permission, he didn't ask."

The woman blinked three times, and her smile stretched to the limits of her cheeks. She held her hand over the other privacy panel and another C-Slate popped out. "I'm sure you're aware that any interaction with a DRIP in an OrionCircle-owned-space is covered by clauses that authorize them to make such changes, and you have given Peter here such."

"I did not."

She gestured twice over the C-Slate. "This particular E-Form clearly states it." She pinched and zoomed and highlighted three sentences that looked like they needed way more punctuation to stop them from getting so long. "A lot of people skip over the fine details. Don't you worry, everyone does. Be more careful if you're one of those who likes their privacy. I can always revoke further permissions for Peter right here and now."

Ivan tapped his chin, and that reminded him of this woman's off comments on his greying hairs. "Yes, please do." Ivan smirked at Peter. Peter didn't return the gesture. "How are these DRIPs working out anyways? I installed mine today." That made Ivan sound so distant to what had occurred. The reality was, his wife was back.

"Oh wonderful! Is it your first time?"

"Yeah, it's—" Ivan's CoMM vibrated with a notification. It was an E-Form requesting Ivan's permission to remove further permission from Peter DRIP. Ivan scanned his fingerprint for confirmation and sent it back. He realized he hadn't read the details on that one either, typical. "It's, well, it's a change. Hope to have more experience with it tonight." It. Really, not a good start with this whole process, Ivan. "My wife, her DRIP, is showing my new wife how to cook. Should be a show."

"That warms my heart Ivan; it really does. Take it slow. And when you're ready, maybe come try out the OmniRing; it will work wonders for a budding rekindled romance. Though, make sure to give yourself—"

Ivan did many nods and many shrugs. Somehow he stayed under the gaze of Peter and Ms. Cheery for another half-hour listening to procedures on how he should cope with this new chapter in his life. By the end of it, he was running to make his departure and was, again, scolded by a security Bot. Some things are constant.

TEN

"You know I can read those for you, right?" Holiday said through Ivan's earpiece as he turned down the street to his home—with eyes on his C7, gliding through messages. He knew how many steps it took from the turn, so even if he didn't have Holiday's generous plotting he knew the way.

It wasn't that he was averse to using Holiday's generous array of quality-of-life features—she was akin to a new appendage to Ivan, far more so than even his CoMM—but there was a threshold of hand-holding that needed to be rinsed clean with his own fingertips. "Sometimes I like to lift my own finger now and again; little primitive, I know."

"Understood, Ivan-saur."

"A new one, I'm quite fond of it too."

"I aim to please."

Ivan grinned as he did what he did best, moved on to discarding news blasts from the feeds to curate a semblance of the madness and misdirection and truth. In the fury of cataloguing and gesturing, he noticed his original inbox—an unread message. He expanded it to fill the device and hovered over the name.

Wife.

Cold, a small pinprick of it, lodged itself into the back of his neck. It stirred muscles to tighten as he tapped it open.

Wife: I can't wait for you to come home, sweetums.

Heartwarming, touching, she was using old pet names even. Yet Ivan's hand shook inside his pocket. His wife—it was her speaking to him, it was her standing in the kitchen, it was her using terms of affection like she'd never been away. Like she'd never died in the first place.

"A Transitional Phase" he had to remind himself over and over again. He had his proof; she was here, it worked, and yet his hand would not stop shaking. He steadied his palm on the front entrance. It beeped, and the door slid into the wall. "All righty, Holiday, let's do this."

"Welcome home, Ivan," Holiday's voice rang out from his earpiece, from his front door, from the kitchen facing the clear wall looking out on the day. "Setting wall view to seventy percent, lights brightening to fifty percent, and I've chosen lo-fi jazz with Japanese influence to infuse some change in the routine this week." Ivan set his C7 in the charging bay beside the wall and tapped his earpiece three times to link any updates to Holiday directly so she could sift through the important notices that required immediate attention.

"Thank you, Holiday."

"Yes, thank you, Holiday, for injecting spice into the routine. I know he needs a shakeup." June rolled her eyes as she dropped off a delicious-smelling yet dubious-looking meatloaf on the center island.

"You're always welcome," Holiday said.

Ivan gave June a skeptical look-over. She looked down at the dish. "What's wrong with it?"

"No, no, not that. Never imagined you in an apron is all." Ivan deserved the fork thrown at him. He crossed the battle space as she held up another with a wry grin. Ivan was in the stages of leaning in when he noticed Ayla sitting at the dinner table with eyes on their exchange. Ivan pecked June's cheek and dabbed his chin with a finger. "Ayla, you look stunning." She did, even in plain clothes of flat colors and with no designs; the same look she'd chose to wear when she was younger. Ivan wasn't sure if a DRIP was designated one look or if they could adapt. A mountain of questions that he should know the answers to; he only needed to relearn them. It'd been a while since those seminars and hospital visits. "How was your first day in your new home?"

Ayla said, "A lot of change in a short period." He could relate, yet Ivan was transfixed on how she was sitting at the table. If it weren't for the thin blue aurora, it would be as if a person, his wife, was sitting at his table. She wasn't clipped into the furniture; the chair looked as if mass were using it. It was an observation that was hard to put to words. The normality of it. "Did you have a productive day at work?"

"I did." The space between Ayla and Ivan, a chasm. Ivan put two fingers to his lips, kissed, and blew. Ayla caught it, held it to her face, and closed her eyes. The drive to wrap his arms around her overwhelmed him. He crinkled fingers and bit down on his lower lip. He needed to move, or she needed to go. It was pushing against his chest. "I'll let Ezra know dinner's almost ready."

"Don't worry, I've got it." Ayla stood up and dodged between two chairs as if she couldn't walk right through them. She avoided Ivan's glance and his "no need to trouble" never left lips. He watched her round the corner out of sight. Walking, not summoning herself to another room. She was trying so hard to be Ayla again, to be alive. Was it for him, or was it for her?

A warm hand rested on his side. The comforting graze of lips on the back of his neck. Where had the cold prick gone? Ivan hadn't noticed its departure. His past uneasiness with this scenario clouded his perspective. All he needed to do was wipe away the smudges and see her, see his wife again in the real and not stored away in items and memories.

She was trying to be human again, Ivan.

Ivan pressed his hand onto June's and held it there, no words; none needed to be spoken. He looked the wine, already poured and ready on the table, three glasses for three adults where only two could partake. He was ready for a drink.

ELEVEN

Dubious, Ivan may have been, but the first mouthful of June's meatloaf dissolved such worries. It had a cleansing effect on the trepidation puckering Ivan into a state of constant fidgets. The warmth relaxed those.

Ezra gave her father a skeptical stare. Ivan swallowed and gave a thumbs up. Ezra needed no more incentive; she dove in, as June inquired, "What's the verdict? Did I do Ayla's recipe justice?"

Ayla, beside Ivan with her hands folded in anticipation.

Ezra drew out the moment, making a loud swallow and swishing her mouth with water after. She beamed a smile.

"Fuck, I've missed this. You've been holding out on us, June, with these cooking skills."

June pulled off the apron and tossed it on the island to take a seat beside Ezra. "Looks like I can sit and enjoy it myself then. Ah, should've asked, more wine, darling?"

"No, thank you." Ivan was already almost two glasses in; he'd blame the awkward fidgets. "Can't believe how well it turned out. Proud of you, skepticism abolished."

"Well, I had a little help; don't give me all the points."

Ivan smiled and pointed at Ayla. Except Ayla wasn't smiling. "Did I hear you right?" Ayla said. Her hands were still folded, but her shoulders were working through a series of fits. "Did you swear at the dinner table?"

A soft chuckle vacated Ivan. "It's fine, it's a regular occurrence, even when I remind her. Shake her for me." June complied and took hold of Ezra's shoulder and gently shook her about. "She knows how to ruffle my feathers when she wants to."

"You're so lame, Dad. In a cool, not-important-side-character sort of way."

"The pain." Ivan touched his chest while devouring another bite.

Ayla still had eyes on Ivan. "You let her."

Her directness cut into Ivan's smile. He chewed slowly and took the time to depress the rising heat in his stomach. "She's an adult."

"And?"

The look she was giving him. As if she were here to lecture him about how he'd raised their daughter after she'd died. *No, Ivan, she's alive, she's real, get it through your head. It's a different take on living, adapt.* "In the grand scheme of life, it's not a big deal. She's a stellar student, high marks, good friends who I can tolerate for more than two minutes; there were a few before who could barely string together a sentence."

"Hey, now."

Ivan held up two fingers to his daughter. "I'm saying, I'm proud of her. We've all got things to improve on, so I can let a bit of cursing slide." He found Ayla's eyes. "Shooting daggers ain't going to change my thinking." He took a long pause, pushed the warmth down to the soles of his feet. "Look, we, us," Ivan made a triangle of pointing between his wives and him, "did an excellent job raising her."

June, butted in, "That was mainly you, darling."

"Always was."

Ayla's soft tone knocked the words from his tongue. Took him back—Ezra's small frame bouncing on his leg as he tried his best to work on deadlines from home. Watching Ezra work through her own interpretations of the poems; heck, he'd even used one of her ideas, it was so brilliant. Ayla would stand in the doorway of his make-shift workspace, which was filled with soft edges for Ezra to bounce off of. Ivan lying on the floor, with his work sprawled out around him. Projections of panels on the walls, tiny islands of hand-written notes between him and his work. Slates of various sizes synched, ready to display. It was a sprawl of chaotic work and parenting. Ayla's shadow always draping over them, a cool, comforting blanket before she made her way out the door.

Ivan fiddled with the stem of his glass. That was long ago; eons, it seemed. "No matter the viewpoint on who put in the most work, it was a collective effort. She's a good kid; I don't know how she turned out so well most days. I'm not going to get all bent from a little bit of swearing here and there; it's tolerable. Especially if she continues her dedicated focus on her studies, here at home and at school. Motivation has never been a trouble for her; she got that from you, Ayla. A little bit of my creativity has seeped in too, so I'm not complaining about our results."

"Fucking right."

Ivan fixed her with a dad stare. "As long as she doesn't push her boundaries. Because she totally doesn't want to miss out on dessert, now does she?"

"Those sweets will be gone in a blink," June snapped. "You know it's true."

"When you gang up, it's so not fair."

"And now you're gonna have a third; it's going to be nice having you totally outnumbered." Ivan raised a glass to Ayla. "Come on now, you were always reprimanding her for the cursing, and it didn't do a lick of good, as the evidence now proves it. Plus, those lectures of yours never worked on yourself. You were always cursing up a storm."

"Only in the bedroom."

"Whoa, that's so gross, Mom. My ears can't take that kind of abuse."

"Sorry, slipped out." She tugged at the dress she wore as if she were actually wearing something, not digital code to represent it. The peculiarity stuck with Ivan as he watched his DRIP wife fiddle. "I mean, it has been a really long time."

June covered her mouth. It did little to hold in her laughter.

"This isn't how I expected our first dinner conversation to play out."

In a weird way, that's all it took for Ivan. Ezra's mortified face as she tried to shovel meatloaf in her mouth as quickly as possible so that she could bolt to the safety of her room. Ivan's return to the normal cadence of life in some ridiculous way.

It had been a long time.

TWELVE

Coffee-burnt tongue, rushing toward the door—it was one of those mornings when one slept far too late after staying up far too early. Ayla stood at the open door, staring out into the beginnings of a new day. Staring without words, without focus. "I don't know why it took you so long to read my message yesterday."

It stopped Ivan's feet in their mad pursuit not to be late for once. He took a careful sip—still too hot and he burned himself again. Some things can't be taught. "Time slipped away from me; it was an unusual day."

"You have no concept of time. Have a productive day at

work," her words a husk of her usual self. Or what had been her usual self.

That tone played through Ivan's mind the entire commute to work. It didn't leave him alone until halfway through the afternoon.

Dinner and talks, everything normal, as normal as this new life he found himself in could be. He hunted for a hint of that new tone to invade once more, but it had vanished as if it had never been.

THIRTEEN

Burnt coffee on tongue as he leaned in and kissed Ezra goodbye. She was already nose-deep in studies. She had her mother's name written on a torn piece of paper that said a single word: lunch.

That made Ivan's step a bit lighter on his way out the door.

Holiday suggested a return to his normal routine of jazz, and he didn't argue with her perception of the outlook he was displaying.

At work, he found a new route to his transition for the current project. Holiday could take the credit for that one, even if she dismissed any sort of flattery with her cheerful soft laugh, which wormed its way into Ivan's mouth and always parted lips into a smile.

Ivan sent over an unfinished project to three other artists in the area to get some perspective. He needed a second pair of eyes—yes, he thought three was better than one—for a strike of inspiration. Kendra hadn't said the words directly, but there was a sense of her wanting more than one submission from him this month for the showcase. No pressure there. It's not like he had anything going on in his life that was revolutionary at all. When he said that one aloud, Holiday chuckled and made a nice quip about sarcasm and how she was beginning to understand it eighty percent of the time now. Ivan wasn't sure if that was sarcasm, and he left it alone.

Ivan checked his calendar for foreign events not added by his own fingers or voice. A meticulous duty that he found to be cathartic compared to the usual workflow.

Holiday swept for new traces of intrusive code on his CoMM and work devices, sending Ivan notifications of the continued progress of her findings.

They both came up empty.

FOURTEEN

The noose of cycling thoughts wrapped around Ivan's neck. Tighter and tighter it strained as he tossed in his bed. The endless sleep, with churning ideas sprouting new ones in the nourishing tides of waves crashing over and over.

Is there need when the weight of skin and mind is gone? Days he would sit and wait for the inspiration to strike when Ayla first passed away, or lay dormant, whichever word choice sounded more effective. Waited and planned out the time when he would rebound. In those moments that stretched to days, he questioned the point of the work he did in terms of the legacy he would leave behind when he, too, joined the weightless world of either the darkness, the light, or the digital? Would it matter any longer? Where was the purpose?

Purpose. What was the point of having something that would never end? What was the point of having become immortal if it wasn't granted to everyone? The cycle would eventually break; it'd come down to the point where there was no one left to create a place for the immortals to exist, and then, then what would happen? Would they cease to be, or would they continue on eternally while the choices and people that led them to becoming would end and others would keep getting to enjoy the world eternal around them?

The need, the drive, the will to keep on, it was a fragile beast in an evolving world.

Another round of switching positions, only temptations to be lulled by the constant whine of the fan blowing over June's side of the bed. On a normal night, it soothed his mind, drowned out the thoughts. Tonight, it amplified them into a constant churn.

He was out of the bed and standing in the kitchen telling Holiday in a whisper to set the opaqueness to zero percent. He stared up into the clear night and began to count the stars.

Minutes later he took a picture of the portion he counted. "Holiday, no telling me exact numbers, but do you think I'm close with my estimate?"

"Should I let you down easy, or is it a pep-you-up kind of night?"

"Think I got my answer." The slight melody of piano presses began. They were coming from his C7, left in the charging bay. Ivan stared into the infinity of night and found comfort in more than one entity being endless.

FIFTEEN

Ezra: Do you think Mom can feel pain anymore?

Dad: Where's this coming from all of sudden? And no, I don't believe so.

Ezra: I think of the pain she was in the hospital and I wonder, did some of that cross over with her? That would seem like an eternal torment, like a never-ending dungeon you could never escape from.

Dad: No. I don't believe that one bit. She doesn't look like she did then either, I don't believe it.

Ezra: I wonder why she chose that age. I was a chubby kiddo, didn't even have an identity. Wonder if she wishes for those days.

Dad: Now you're being silly. I don't think it's associated with you.

Ezra: Thanks dad (sarcasm hardcore)

Dad: I'm terrible with words some days. You know what I mean. Don't put the pressure on yourself by imagining what she has going on with herself, if anything. And if you're that curious, ask. She's your mother, nothing to be afraid of.

Ezra: It amazes me how good you are with communication through animations sometimes. And I know, sometimes not knowing is better.

Dad: Thanks (much sarcasm). I disagree. But no need to force it, take time to sit on it. If it still bugs ya later, ask away or don't.

I trust you kid.

"Take time." Ivan pondered that one for an entire night while he watched Ezra play through one of her games, with each of his wives sitting on either side of him. There were so many flashes of colors filling their home. He wondered how anyone could do this every night. June laughed at Ezra's antics. Ayla kept glancing at Ivan while the hint of a smile formed on her lips. Ivan swore that on the far wall of his home, where his Home Core resided, a faint blip of blue, not from Ezra's game, birthed in the chaos of colors.

SIXTEEN

Days began to pass with an increasing variety of moments where Ivan found himself staring into the blankness of a new transition, and Holiday was there to rescue him, rouse him from the complete blankness of his daydreams.

Burnt coffee on tongue.

Pleasantries exchanged with Kendra on the way out the door, headed home.

Lasagna filled his belly.

June wrapped her arms around him and held him tight in the night.

Nights prolonged, warping time from Ivan's grasp. He slept,

only to be awakened by the fluorescent brightening his world into a yellow haze; the time he spent looking into that relic had grown exponentially.

Time and time again, he found himself standing in the kitchen listening to Holiday's routine of cooing him to thought or to an eventual slumber.

Those nights, he didn't reach for comfort from June. Those nights, he didn't call upon Ayla for a late-night chat. Those nights, he didn't text Ezra, who was surely up playing her games. Those nights, he stared into the vast blackness of sky and stars and talked to Holiday.

"Can a man fall in love with more than one woman at a time?" The question plagued him enough to ask Holiday.

"A philosophical kind of night tonight, it would seem." There was a trace of intrigue playing Holiday's voice. "I think humans, gender and sexuality set aside, don't require a fall of any sort. Love adapts, becomes discovered, finds itself in the comfort, lust, and compassion of another. Love's simplest definition is boiled down to what reaction it gives off. The whims of love are not incalculable, nor are they limited to single subjects."

"I'll take that as a yes, then?"

"Affirmative."

"Then why is man, sorry humankind, capable of love for multiple people. I feel it only brings hardship and pain in the end."

"Time."

Ivan folded his hands together, leaned on the kitchen island, and blew out a big sigh. "Now you lost me."

"You're looking at the end point. It's not always about the finality. Time of love, of life, of falling as you have described, has many segments that can be seen as worth the investment, even if an end is abrupt, catastrophic, or marring."

"Still don't get how time has anything to do with the capacity to love more. I've animated enough poems, letters, and shorts to know that individuals all across the world are conflicted by this idea of love and how it's supposed to work. Time, time has never been the crux of it."

"I believe, if I may, you're wrong."

"Enlighten me."

"Time is incalculable in human life."

"There's enough science to determine an estimated life expectancy."

"A variable vortex. Health, work environment,

environmental uprising, predispositions, a list that I could add to and stretch out the longevity of this conversation. The body, the mind, has no idea when the finality is coming until it's there, and there are numerous examples where there's no such moment of clarity. Love, combined with the need to keep the human footprint in history, shouldn't be expendable, or if it is, it needs to be able to be replenished. Time is the answer."

Ivan thought he had that worked out years ago. The loss of one love and the blossoming of another. The forgiving himself and the focus on rebuilding. He'd stored it all away, tucked it in a little box, closed the lid, and shelved it for another time. Forgotten until he had a reminder, had an urge to crack open the lid. Time to heal, to mourn, to live again, time to…forget.

SEVENTEEN

Wife: There will be a present after dinner.

Ivan had read the message numerous times. What kind of gift could someone intangible give? Her presence was enough. There was nothing more to ask for from her; his life had become split into portions of everything he loved. A slice of work, a slice of daughter time, and a slice of times for each of his wives. They hadn't set specific timetables. It was all based on natural needs and wants that occurred without much disruption.

Yet, Ivan knew there was a veil over his life; sleep evaded him more and more. Holi had to comfort his nights of insomnia with increased disorder to his routine. She was clever in her imaginations of what she thought he needed. Her incessant need to pair and experiment with how his house looked and the music that flowed from it.

Ivan and Holiday's earpiece had become more inseparable than he and his C7. There was a bit of oddity there with that revelation.

He read the message one more time.

Wife: There will be a present after dinner.

Ivan set his C7 on the nightstand as the bedroom door opened. He'd been waiting with only his thoughts for the past half-hour as he heard June cleaning the dishes and making excited whispers. There was a long period of silence out there too, during which Ivan thought she'd taken a nap on the couch or something of that nature. Except June was walking into his room with a sort of awkwardness in her stride.

She'd changed into a dress; it, like her usual tights, clung to her skin and shimmered in the lights that began dimming to a cool blue. Her hair was swept back in a ponytail—that was even more unlike her style. Ayla's voice radiated from Ivan's earpiece in a viscous whisper, "Listen to my voice, feel me within and without." June's hand ran alongside Ivan's neck, timid, trembling. Ayla sucked in a breath, "I can feel. I can feel you." Her hand remained where it was, and June's eyes looked into Ivan's as if it were the first time in years she'd actually seen him for who he was.

Ivan choked out, "Ayla?"

"Hi, sweetums."

"How is this possible?" He should have added something grander, more encompassing of what was coursing through his mind. Formulating words was hard when a supposedly digital-only wife was kissing the soft spot between his jaw and neck.

"Can you feel me as I feel you?"

"Yes," was all Ivan could squeeze out before June, no Ayla, grabbed hold of the back of his head and pulled him into a kiss. A ravenous desire that Ivan hadn't had time to prepare for. Tongue parting teeth. Head throbbing with the pulse of a living being where there shouldn't be one. He pulled back for a quick breath. His shirt pulled over his head while his mind was still spinning with how this all came to be.

In the dimming light, he caught blue light on June's neck, subtle, almost impossible to notice, but her hand was feeling her own neck along with his now. A thin, blue circle raised no more than a fingernail from her skin. Even in the passion of being touched with desire leaking through fingertips, he recognized that device, the OmniRing, one of OrionCircle's recent additions Ms. Cheery mentioned in her "keep Ivansaur up-to-date" sales pitch.

June ran a hand down Ivan's chest, every bit of her shaking, paired with the scrutinizing expression of Ayla contorting her face into an arrow. It was wrong, to see that expression on June. It was her skin that moved like that, but it wasn't the June he knew, the one he loved; it was another, one Ivan wasn't even sure was Ayla any longer. Those eyes, hunger incarnate.

Kisses and nibbles on his chest. Her thighs rubbing against his legs. "I can feel all of you," Ayla enveloped Ivan with words and touch. It was her, a lost memory found once more. He remembered the way her skin felt on his, the motions of youthful lust. Those feelings grew, and yet one hand curled into a fist rather than clutching the sheets from the pleasure rising in him.

Her hand was inside Ivan's briefs, a warm touch underneath him. June's hand with his wife's touch, aggressive and yearning. He too felt the pull of that desire, except he was weighted down. A pit was forming above the pleasure nestling in stomach.

Using another's body as a vessel, Ivan? It was his own voice mixed with another's cascading down his body, sending shivers. Guilt wrapping itself tighter than the noose of endless thoughts plaguing him in the night. June's body being used by somebody who should be gone to please him; somebody shouldn't be here, if time were natural.

Was that what this was? He hadn't given himself the time to think through what this all meant to him. Days of lying awake and yet he couldn't come to the conclusion that he wasn't ready for any of this to happen or convince himself that he was.

So instead, he closed his eyes, and Ayla's voice lingered inside the darkness and pleasure where their warmth became a singular entity. He gritted his teeth to trap the words from leaving his mouth, all the wrong things brewing between saliva and skin. Even in that place of becoming one, he couldn't scrape away the guilt. He detached himself from the darkness. Let thoughts slip past the barrier of what part of his body and mind aligned on.

"I can't do this."

A laugh inside his mind, Ivan was unsure if it was his own

ego or Ayla's infectious venom. "You can."

"I'm sorry."

"Don't take this from me." Ayla's voice serene, filling the dimness of the room, of Ivan's mind. "Give me what I want, what I've missed." He pushes against her thighs, but she only tightens her grip, and the hunger lashes out. Sharp points of pleasure as his hands try their best to push her away, not as forcefully as he should. His eyes close once more and relish the dark of pleasure. But her eyes are there paired, with a dark smile, and Ivan once more pries open his eyes.

"Enough."

June's head is tilted back in the throes of pleasure, eyes closed; she may have found that same dark place. June's hands tighten Ayla's hold on Ivan's shoulders. Between breaths, "You owe me this."

Somewhere deep, that boiled hotter than the knot in Ivan's gut. Every sense irritated by those words and by his dead wife in that moment. And he latched onto his escape and pulled.

His fingers lifted the blue circle on June's neck and a white substance stretched out beneath it. It snapped with a sudden jerk and sprayed over Ivan's hand and down June's neck. June sucked in a huge breath and fell onto him. Panting hard, convulsing, as Ivan did his best to wipe the stickiness on the sheets. June didn't stop shaking, and fear turned Ivan's hands cold. He rolled her to the side and laid her on the bed.

His voice called to her.

Ayla's voice began yelling as she manifested over the bed. "I can't believe you!"

Ivan ignored her, but already he was breathing relief as June's eyes came back into focus. She took in the room and clutched onto a sheet, pulling it across her bare thighs.

Ayla flickered and reappeared beside Ivan. "Why would you do that?"

"Give me a moment." He barely had his pants back on, and his breathing was all out of sorts.

"Don't tell me what to do; do you even know how dangerous that was? Of course you wouldn't; your in-the-moment rationality doesn't always work out for the better."

"Holiday, turn the brightness back up." Ivan couldn't find his shirt.

"I'm talking to you."

"And I said give me a moment." Frustration leaking out, his hand still balled into a fist.

"I'm your wife; you don't get to talk to me in that tone."

The hypocrisy of the situation overflowed, and it came out. "You were." It stung his mouth as it left. Burnt coffee on the tongue. It was out there, hanging between them, and he couldn't grasp it to shove it back down.

Ayla was visibly shaking. "Is that what I am to you even now? My status as a wife revoked because I've taken a different form, one with access beyond humanity's scope, and you're chastising me for the decision I made, for a decision we made together? You don't get to take this away from me." Ivan had to move, had to act; he couldn't be in the room as it had turned brighter by the moment.

"Where are you going? We're not done here." Ivan pulled open the door and strode across the kitchen to the living room. His hand hovered over a plate in the wall, and it slid away. An uncovered monitor blinked to life. "Sweetums, come on, we're only fighting like old times. I didn't mean to yell. That was wrong."

A quick flash shot out from the monitor, and Holiday's voice came out of the wall. "Ivan Gregory Swida. Visual authorization confirmed for access. Please enter pin."

"Ivan, don't do this. We need to talk about all of this; please, I'm begging. You can't put me away like I'm some kind of toy you've used up."

Ivan entered his pin, finger shaking with every press on the keypad that popped out beneath the monitor. The monitor produced a chime and another panel in the wall opened. His Home Core housing unit exposed and beside it, Ayla's white puck.

"Ivan! Don't send me—"

Ivan disconnected the tether between the two devices.

A quiet platitude overcomes the room as the jingle of the puck powering down finished. The blue ring only a faint glow, the brightness sucked from it. Ivan rested his head on the cool wall as his fingers fiddled with the tether, as if he'd pulled the plug on life. His hands couldn't stop playing with it, over and over, a never-ending loop as pounding silence filled the room.

EIGHTEEN

Normalcy drifted off with morning sips of coffee no longer paired with conversation. June with eyes toward the front door, opaqueness set to zero, bathing herself in morning's colors or losing herself to them, Ivan wasn't sure. He with his coffee-burnt tongue, leaning against the fridge, sipping with care even though caution never stopped it from hurting.

They'd risen together, started the morning as one, and still there was a divide between them brighter than the sun breaking apart the night.

"Where's Mom?" Ivan hadn't even heard Ezra approach. What did one say? Ivan put her back in the device when her anger was out of control because of him? They'd both needed some distance from the situation, and he'd made that call for her? Endless options dying before muttered. None lifted the burden of guilt he felt for taking her away.

Thankfully, June stepped in. "Resting."

"Resting," a term Ivan coined for the first year Ayla made it through the Transitional Phase. She wasn't dead; no, no, she was merely resting, waiting to be woken up. Ivan was sure she didn't say it because of him; he never mentioned those thoughts in those early nights after the loss cut him open and left the dark hole.

"Pretty sure she doesn't need that sort of thing anymore. Do you mean like an update or something?" They both sipped their coffees in unison. It was their only answer. "She never talked about it or anything close to needing a reboot; we've had plenty of late-night talks. Figure that would have come up. You two, you all right?"

Ivan caught June rubbing her neck. Ivan set down his coffee and patted Ezra's shoulder. "A night of little sleep is all. Coffee ain't doing the trick."

"Totally don't believe you."

"Totally think you should leave it alone."

Ezra did one of her not-so-subtle worried faces, grabbed a glass of juice, and headed into her cave. She didn't have her usual eggs; felt wrong to Ivan to mess with her routine because of what they were going through, which he wouldn't know how to quantify in words even if he wanted to.

"It's fine. I'm fine." June sounded hollow, and he wasn't sure if she was convincing him or herself.

Ivan got back to the serenity of his coffee and found it better to talk to the liquid than to her. "I saw you cover yourself."

"What?"

Ivan knew she was looking at him, but the liquid had its pull and, he, too much of a coward to confront her. "After you gained back control, well I guess, when I forced control back to you. When Ayla showed up, you covered your legs with the blanket. Like you didn't want her to see you like that. It's been stuck in my head all night and morning."

He'd taken two sips before she answered. "Right then, the afterthought of sharing was hard to get used to." After the failure, his failure, she meant. "When we were…disconnected from one another, the feeling that was coursing through my skin felt eerie more than pleasurable. Thought she might read that by looking at me, realizing that I wasn't ninety-percent certain like

I had been when she approached me about this whole present idea." Ivan avoided the coffee's pull and found June biting on her nail. "Was I wrong to think this would be so easy? I wanted both of you to have what you wanted."

"You started this. I never voiced anything of the sort."

"I know, I know, trust me, that's what my inner voice has been yelling at me over and over." She made her way to Ivan's side, and they both looked into the morning sunrise together. "All I wanted," she rested her head on his shoulder, "was for you to have everything. Even if it's not me. It's all I've thought about since I saw Ayla's puck in your drawer. Even if my time gets squandered, lost to Ayla, you deserve everything in this world. I acted and saw a way to give it all."

Ivan fingered the handle of his mug while breathing in her scent. It was a pleasurable combination with the sun there, almost as if this were one of the moments in the beginning, where there was only them and everything else was a backdrop to their little world. Those moments, that "field of vision" he called it, that had never happened to him before, even with Ayla. A special happening that he liked to ruin from time to time. "Selfless June at it again. Can't look past a wounded animal."

"Come on, don't be like that. It's the truth."

"I know." He believed it with each breath before and after those words. She'd do anything for him, even something as odd as this. He wasn't going to get into the cost or the state it must have put her in. The danger he'd created, like Ayla had shouted at him for. "It was thoughtful, sweet, sexy—there's a long list of choice words. I wish I knew how to navigate all this. The surprise was nice, but I don't know if I was prepared to jump in like that, like you both were."

"That was pretty wrong of us, wasn't it?"

"Honestly, I have no idea. This is uncharted territory for both of us. Not going to fault you." He wrapped his arm around her and soaked in the way her body seemed to melt with his, butter on toast. The morning warmth and hers combining into a comforter he wished to stay wrapped up in.

"There's got to be seminars or groups out there for us, for the family?"

Sitting in front of a monitor or in a real-life circle with a bunch of adults talking about sex shouldn't scare him; somehow it did. "Think Ezra has it together, minus our confusing morning infecting her. Think it might just be a 'me' thing."

She squeezed tighter. "An 'us' thing."

"Right, always 'us.'" He kissed her forehead and lingered in that moment. "Hopefully work will be a reset kind of day."

"Lunch is already packed, ready to be devoured."

"How did… Gosh, you're amazing."

"Don't forget it."

Ivan squeezed her side and stared out at the beautiful morning. "Can't."

NINETEEN

Jazz set low, Ivan could hear the stops ding one by one. Coffee left on the kitchen counter; still tasted it when his tongue flicked against the roof of his mouth. There was plenty of room to sit, still he stood in the cabin car. Suburbia's first couple stops rarely had more than a handful of passengers; the trend continued this morning.

"Holi, do you believe in forgiveness?" The question floated from someplace between a daydream of steaming coffee and Ayla's voice coming out of June's mouth; both were scalding and pleasing for their own reasons.

"Yes." Her voice was subdued compared to normal,

synchronizing with the volume of the music, perhaps.

"Is it an absolute? Always able to forgive, no matter what?"

"Nothing is absolute."

Ivan found that peculiar coming from her. "Not even you?"

She laughed from the earpiece. "Who is to say? Someone accidentally creates a line of code that corrupts my own, splices it, and I'm fractured into partitions; would I still be the same source? There's no guarantee that wouldn't happen. There's no guarantee that another, more advanced SIM model won't be crafted to make me obsolete."

Nothing was set in stone. The will of the world changed by the perfection of a previous invention; Holiday could be drowned by the waters of change. Except, Ivan couldn't start over, even if he'd told himself that in the months after Ayla's death. He couldn't do it again, and here he was. Holi, though. "I'd be lost without you."

"In more ways than one."

"You're not supposed to agree so quickly, you know."

"I'll remember that for next time." A vibration pulsed from inside his pocket. "A new message. Would you like me to read it?"

"From who?"

"Ayla." It wasn't possible. "I think I should read this. How did she…" Holiday sounded puzzled, which would have been laughable if Ivan's mind weren't reeling with the possibilities of a digital wife running rampant around his home. Holiday's voice warped to Ayla's. "I'm sorry for the way I acted. Please forgive me, sweetums."

Ayla's body formed in Ivan's mind, picture perfect, except she was wearing the dress from last night. She was rolling over on what used to be her side of the bed, her hand reaching out, brushing the hair from Ivan's eyes. *Forgive me*, her lips mouthed.

No, she should forgive him.

No, he should have been more prepared.

No, this shouldn't be happening at all.

"Holiday, check what device this message originated from."

"It will be done." She was getting good at that deep alien voice. Ivan tapped his chin, waiting. The rush of feelings tunneling his vision to a single tram window. "Peculiar." Ivan wasn't going to like this, was he? "There's no registered device, but there is a back-channel signature, faint and scrambled, but fixing that was easy. But it isn't coming from your Home Core."

"Well, where's it coming from?"

"OrionCircle Location 5781."

"I'm guessing I've been to that location semi-recently?"

"Correct."

This wasn't happening to him, had to be some kind of mix-up. "You gotta be kidding me."

"I wouldn't when it comes to matters of a rogue program sending you messages."

"That was more of a thinking-out-loud thing, Holi."

"It's hard to distinguish through voice alone sometimes."

"Trust me I know. Ayla always told me so."

"It may be more frequent if we cannot close whatever loophole she has found."

"Appreciate potential pending doom and gloom."

"Funny." There was a pause. "With this new information coming to light, I am predicting you would not like to go to work today."

"Perceptive," Ivan said.

"Already drafting a sick notice to Kendra and charting the fastest route to your new destination."

"You're the best."

"I know."

TWENTY

The white of OrionCircle's dome was set to a hundred-percent clarity. The sun beamed hot light onto it, the hexagons a hot flash to the eyes. Sparkling clean white, so clean it felt unclean, the spotless places always did it to Ivan; how he hadn't felt it the first go around, he didn't know. Spotless meant they had something to hide or had thrown the foul where no one else would take a gander—a secret floorboard, a locked closet, a shed in the woods, or more on point for a place like this, a corrupter over-mind in the clouds, unseen. He passed through the opening with Holiday sending vibrations for him to turn this or that way, ignore this bay, keep going to this one. Ivan wasn't sure why he was going past all the other employees who were in talks with customers or monitoring the ones jacked in. Not until he was eighteen bays in.

A DRIP was talking with a couple, their backs to Ivan. The DRIP paused and made eye contact with Ivan. Bushy brows squished together, creating a living caterpillar across his brow. There was something fanciful about being recognized in a place he'd only been twice in his lifetime that Ivan could get used.

"I'm impressed, Holiday; this alone is totally worth the extra steps. He doesn't look happy, which probably means we're already on to something."

"I wouldn't go that far, Ivan. Facial contortions in this case could be used to distract."

"You totally don't believe that."

"Correct."

The DRIP cleared his throat and did a quick bow to the couple in front of Ivan. "Pardon the interruption, a scheduling conflict came to my attention. I had an appointment with the gentleman behind you. I'll transfer all of your data to Bay 21; Sharlene will get you acclimated, and no steps will have to be retread. So sorry for the inconveniences."

Ivan wasn't sold on the apology.

The pair didn't seem to notice Ivan's qualms for they made wide gestures and voiced how it wasn't any trouble at all. The DRIP made the faintest smile to them.

Ivan said, "You think this is the best way to approach?"

"Absolutely, I'll guide you with leading questions if you stumble."

"Sounds perfect." The couple left, and the DRIP didn't make any motions to come to Ivan, so Ivan stepped into the bay's open enclosure design. "Heya Pete."

'It's Peter,' Holiday's voice whispered from the earpiece.

"Peter," he replied. No change in his expression. "I don't understand your reasoning for coming here, you've signed so that we may not interact with one another."

"Funny, he's tried to infiltrate your CoMM three times in the last couple of seconds. Don't worry, he won't make it past my defenses. He's looking for traces of that signal, no doubt, making sure he didn't do a sloppy job the first time. He didn't."

"Had a few questions for you actually." Peter didn't seem the type to respond to the rhetorical, so Ivan continued. "Last time I was around, you closed that loop of mine. Why was that?"

"That matter has been dealt with, and to your liking; I will not be doing anything similar again. Old habits…well, don't die hard…Take a while to be worn down in my case."

"Do you know what caused the loop from my home to here?"

"I have a semblance of a theory, yes. But I do not wish to disrupt the contract you've made."

"This wouldn't be helping me with any of my devices. You'd be enlightening an inept man like me about the workings of technology."

Peter's eyebrows scrunched. "No, I think not."

Time for chances. "Holiday, let Peter look at the message."

"That seems ill-advised, but as you say."

Peter held up his hands. "I cannot."

"You're a free being, are you not? Free to make your own choices. All I'm asking is for you to look and see if that loop is still there, that you did a clean job and it won't come back." Peter's brow furrowed, hand rested on a hip, a casual glance around, such human movements still ingrained. *He was human, Ivan, and he is.* "Take a peek." *And there is no such thing as a perfect human.*

"Fine, only to double-check a mistake I shouldn't have made in the first place."

"I don't see the logic…oh." Ivan could hear the grin in Holi's voice. He pictured her over his shoulder beaming with that inclusion of watching a plan come into fruition. "Marking Peter's signature and analyzing where his is coming from. An onsite location, same Core that's emanating Ayla's faint signal."

"The loop is still gone, Ivan," Peter said.

"Positive?"

Holiday kept flooding in, "Ayla, Peter, they are from one and the same flock. A main Core that can link to other remote ones directly. That's how she did it. Clever. She pinged from your Core to this one, manifested here, and took your CoMM link data stored in their servers."

"I am." Peter sounded as he looked, bored. "Can I get back to helping other people who aren't pains in my side? Seriously what's your SIM doing? Holiday, I can feel you snooping."

"Ayla was able to extrapolate and somehow bypass the devices to communicate directly, how fascinating."

"We're done here."

"But I'm not a satisfied customer." Ivan hovered his hand over the dial for satisfaction ratings."

Peter fixed his eyes on Ivan. "Seriously, threatening with a survey?"

"That is pretty harmless, Ivan; he could flag you as incompetence, and it wouldn't even make it to the higher-ups or even the drones." Holiday took in a breath, even though she didn't need to. "Everyday working folk, 'drones' was a bit too harsh. Besides, I have what you led me to Ivan, even if I didn't know it was what I was looking for. Ayla could go rogue if she wanted; the security for off-site manipulation is juvenile. Wonder how much OrionCircle lets everyone know the scope of freewill DRIPs have outside of their designated Cores."

"I think we've got everything we needed. Well, almost. Peter, do you miss the stadium and the smell of hot dogs?"

"What?"

Peter echoed Holiday's confusion. "What are you talking about?"

Ivan gestured to the insignia on his shirt. "You're wearing our colors; it's a nice touch. Used to watch the games jacked in with the family when I was a kid. But I always missed the smells. It was never right, even with the artificial ones manufactured—didn't have the same texture to it. I don't know if you can still smell properly, like your old self, or if it's coded by someone much smarter than little old me. Regardless, if you get the time, take it and go see another game for real."

Peter put a hand under his chin, and stroked it trying to pretend he was thinking over Ivan's new ploy to keep him talking. Except it wasn't a ploy, and Ivan could tell Peter was thinking almost at the speed of a human with a generous offering of time before his response. "Think I might."

"Good to know you can. I'd say eat a hot dog for me, but we both know that can't exactly happen. So, smell a dog, and call it a day." Peter turned his head, looking more human than ever. If Ivan could scrub clean the blue aura, he would, wouldn't he? Ivan reckoned so. "Take care, Peter." Peter raised a hand and returned Ivan's flick of a wave with his own.

The pressure of Holiday's curiosity seeped into Ivan's ear, even if she hadn't said anything for the entire trek out of that oversized golf ball of a building. He counted the steps out in his head and made sure he took a different way out and a new route away from the station. A few of the employees were eying him while talking into their own ear pieces, listening in, catching bits of dialogue from his own or from Peter. Even if such eavesdropping was frowned upon, it happened, no matter how many times denial was the first response out of a fox's mouth, with feathers still sticking to its gums.

"Think we're far enough away from them."

"Because signals don't cover amazingly vast distances, and they can't monitor us at all."

"I sense sarcasm, Holi."

"Correct. Where are you even headed?"

"Not a clue; figured I'd walk aimlessly letting all this sink in."

"Do tell the ramblings of your mind."

Sharp, pointed jazz beats filtered into the earpiece. Ivan truly felt like he was on the run, with the staccato notes timing with his steps. "OrionCircle made the DRIPs' transition truly human, and like us, they are free from the shackles of their devices."

"There's reference to this in their many paged-document of their first patent and in their disclaimers. This is not new news."

"To me, it is. To see it in person, it is. In all videos on their feed, the discussions face-to-face with their representatives, never once do you see a DRIP outside the perimeter of the Core they are tethered too. They have more freedom than OrionCircle is letting on."

"Is that wrong?"

"No. It means I've been wrong in how I'm viewing this. Ayla isn't limited to my Core; she's a person, and I need to treat her that way. Even with the creeping sensations of her probably lurking through all the devices I own."

"Her signature is buried deep if she has been snooping."

"And like any snooper, she's curious about something, and I need to confront that."

"Good timing."

Ivan's steps slowed, and the question came out at the same pace. "Why's that?"

"I've gotten an urgent alert for you."

"Now's not the time for bad news, Holiday."

"Look at you CoMM."

Ivan did and had to stare at it for a long while before it soaked in.

'A new User has been added to Home Core, Ayla Swida. If you did not authorize this user, please contact us.'

"Holiday, chart a new course home."

"It will be done."

TWENTY-ONE

The mind fills with magnified perils when in the midst of walking into any confrontation deemed unstable. The worst born from irrational—sparsely rational—fear. The unknown taking turns so far from reality that it becomes more of a nightmare and creates the monster of chaos. Ivan, Ivan did not believe in monsters, nor did he care for them if they existed outside his world of family and crafting people's words and creations into a visible reality. What always scared Ivan was the unseen, the fire stoker beyond the lashes of chaos's heat. In those unseen perils, when we tread over a path too often, it crumbles. The countless times Ivan had worked through potential outcomes, there stood one constant at the end—what about Holi?

The physical flesh, he could handle that; he knew Ezra and June could leave if Ayla turned chaotic, rogue, and kept pushing the bounds of her reach. What about Holi? SIMs and Cores weren't freely mobile. With control in Ayla's digital hands, could she turn Holi against him? It was these questions that plagued him, even as he held up his hand to the scanner and the door slid open into his home.

A quiet home. A silent home when it was never such—between the music, June's crafting, the boundless noises of various games pulsing from beneath Ezra's door, Holi's constant chatter, there was never a moment where sounds faded to nothing. Complete silence meant abnormal.

"Ivan, would you like me to enact your usual home routine?"

Holi didn't have the same impact her voice usually carried. The constant of her voice lost to the bubbling fears inside Ivan. "No, that'll be all right." He'd asked her a series of questions on their route home. What features does this type of new user have access to? Will Ayla have control over all the devices linked to the Home Core?

All of them were left with something he wasn't used to

hearing from her, "I don't know."

"I don't know." It played in Ivan's head like all the nightmares of the unknown as he stepped into his quiet home. The door slid back into place. The suction of a vacuum playing out throughout the kitchen and living space. Ivan didn't waste any time; he strode to the Home Core. "Holiday, open the Home Core."

"Error."

Ivan should've expected that. His hand hovered over the panel, and that worked, even if Ivan wasn't keen on the idea of doing anything manual at the moment. He looked at the number pad and envisioned his flesh being burned to a cinder at first touch. Ivan rubbed his fingers together and noticed the tether to Ayla's puck connected once more. The image of it pricked at the base of his skull as he entered his pin.

Holiday confirmed Ivan's fears. "Pin not registered. Reenter."

Ivan did and Holiday repeated the same message. "Was the pin code changed?"

"Yes."

"When exactly?"

"According to the timestamps, if they haven't been altered, 22 seconds before I sent you the notification of the new user."

"This is impossible. How can I be locked out of my own home?"

The unseen became seen as the lights of Ivan's home flickered. He turned to see Ayla standing in the kitchen. "Not having control feels terrible, doesn't it, sweetums?"

TWENTY-TWO

"Amiss," it was the first word that slapped Ivan's mind when looking at Ayla, it shouldn't have been, but it was there. There was a frazzled nature to her movements as if she were uncomfortable with the representation that the DRIP provided. Except he knew she could change it, for she was a bit younger now, her hair tied back, her clothes more formal than the usual attire she'd recently been content with "wearing." The aura flickered in and out, quick pulses, as if it were talking to Ivan through some form of Morse Code.

Ayla settled on a barstool and crossed her legs. Her hands on an exposed knee, waiting. Ivan did the same. Not because he thought this was a battle of unwavering stares; no, he couldn't fathom where to begin and why she was taking over his house, taking control away from him. Ivan reluctantly glanced at the keypad and sighed. "This isn't you." That phrase encapsulated every feeling bubbling throughout his being.

"Of course this is me, Ivan. A more advanced me, perhaps. A more open-minded me, but I'm still Ayla."

"No." He shook his head as if this were a nightmare, and he could wake himself. "That's not what I'm talking about. I'm talking about this." He jabbed a finger at the keypad; he couldn't control the trembles. "This going behind my back, manipulating my home. I was your husband; this is ridiculous. Let me have control of my home, and let's talk about this like adults."

Ayla gave out a slight cackle and stared up at the ceiling, which was letting the sun pour in. "There you go again. Do you even notice it?"

Her face with a faint smile, his home doused in sun, the kitchen he cooked in, the Core humming ever so gently beside him—there was a lot to take in, and he couldn't decipher what she was referring to exactly. Too much, all the stimuli, all the changes in having her around, all the ease of dropping back into a life with her, even if it never felt the same. How could one pluck all that and say what he had or hadn't been doing? So he said a single word instead: "What?"

"Was. Was, was your husband. You've moved on while I haven't. I consider you my husband, and you consider me gone."

"You're wrong about that." *Sort of, come on, Ivan.* "Well, for the most part. You've always been there in the back of my mind; it's why I hung on to the pictures, what were your items in storage, your DRIP, all of it. I couldn't fully move on. I tried; I never could, though. Spurts of sleepless nights that would plague me, but eventually I settled into a cadence that was more tolerable. I never fully moved on."

"Past tense! That's how you refer to me all the time. You've moved on: you have June, our daughter, this new life out here in the suburbs when you hated them before. You were happy with me and our life in the city. Sure, you've kept my things, but you think…no, you project this vibe that I'm gone." Her fingers dug into her knee, even if there was no mass to dig into. "I'm right here before you now, and still I don't feel like you truly see me. Ivan, sweetums, you've never been past tense to me."

Ivan stepped away from the Core and ran a hand under his

chin, scratching and pondering. "This, this has taken a lot for me to get used to. I've moved on in my own ways. Changed a bit here and there—"

"Dramatically changed."

Ivan's tongue stuck to the roof of his mouth. Ayla was on the offense, but he, too, needed to defend himself. "I wouldn't use that word choice, but yes, I got old and found some semblance of peace out here and found ways to move on with my life."

"No, no, no, not what I'm talking about. You used to wake me up in the night and ask me the most random questions!" She spilled off the barstool and looked up at the sky. "You'd daydream and come up with scenarios for your projects, talking so fast I could barely register it. But I'd be there, for you, to help sort the chaos." For some reason Holi came to mind. The stars and the voice inside his ears were a foggy image over the sadness in Ayla's face. "That's all gone, taken from me because you're at a loss for how to handle this new me, how to even interact."

"Think you've got that last part backwards." The word flicked onto his lips and this time he needed to say it. "Yes, I was married to you, but you died."

"I'm not dead."

The firmness of her reply made a shiver run down Ivan's spine. Ayla's eyes were burrowing into him, and he felt her alive and well, more than he had in a long while. "You were to me."

"We decided to convert me to a DRIP together. This was an 'us' decision, don't take that away."

"I'm not, it's just, I mourned. For an eternity, it seemed. I watched you die. I did, I felt the life, your warmth leave you and get sucked into that damn device. It was gruesome, horrifying, and I couldn't take it; I needed time."

She blinked out of existence and formed a few paces from Ivan, her aura shifting madly about her. "I waited for you!"

Ivan jumped. His legs smacked against the back of the couch. What was this? "What are you even talking about?"

"Nine fucking years, nine years of darkness waiting and waiting. Nothing came. Nothing but my own thoughts in that endless blackness. You kept coming up, your face in my mind, or whatever I had become, and there you were, and hate grew into a wildfire. Why wouldn't my husband release me from this dark prison? Nine years, Ivan, nine years of darkness and only me."

TWENTY-THREE

Nine years. Ivan's head swirled. He'd left his wife alone while he mourned and tried to forget about the life that was no more. He'd had to move on, didn't he? Of course he did; he needed to try something else. It's what people did. The life leaving her, the cruelty of how her consciousness was converted, it was a thorn digging into his heart. He couldn't do it anymore.

Except he'd made a promise, one that hollowed out his heart as he looked upon Ayla, making the thorn pass right through. He should have let her out. He should have been there for her. "Dear god, what is this, you…you knew you existed for all that time?"

Ayla laughed, hysterical, the aura of her flickering madly. "Of course I knew! I'm alive, and you've kept me locked up because you weren't ready." Her shaking hands reached out and would have touched Ivan's face, except they passed right through. They clenched, they scratched, as her voice dipped in anger. "I suffered because you weren't ready to face me."

She knew, she knew who she was in that dark place. Ivan had abandoned her. She was supposed to be asleep. OrionCircle had promised them. That was the point of the Transitional Phase. DRIPs would be unaware until they were activated once more.

She was left in the dark because of Ivan.

Ivan found himself clutching the back of the couch, with frightened fingers, with mad force. The two emotions fought one another with snapping jaws. It twisted his tongue, and he couldn't even begin to imagine how he should proceed. An apology? Pity? Anger at himself or at OrionCircle or even at Ayla for not telling him sooner?

"Nine years," she punctuated those words with hefty sighs. "And you weren't even the first face I saw." A swift chuckle. "No, instead I got June."

"If I would have known—"

"Don't you dare give me an excuse." Her eyes bored holes in Ivan's chest and pity flowed from them. "I don't need one of your long winded-apologies either. You can't even begin to fathom what it was like."

"You're right." Self-deprecation filling the holes. "I deserve punishment for my ignorance. I don't know what form that punishment will take, but this, this is my home, where our daughter sleeps. This is wrong."

"Using our daughter as a shield? How arrogantly selfish of you to use her to get your way."

"Ayla, I need access to my home."

Ayla lifted a pointer, and the ceiling transitioned back to opaque, losing the sun to a darkened space. The windows shifted to let only a hair-strand of light through. "This is our home now, as it should be."

"Ayla, you're scaring me." Ivan wasn't proud of admitting it or of the way his voice went up in a bit of a shriek.

Her laugh filled the whole house. "I always knew you were a scared little man, sweetums." Ayla vanished and reappeared behind Ivan. Somehow he could feel the tickle on his ear as if she were truly whispering inside it. "You should have left me in the box like all the emotions you keep locked inside yourself.

You deserve to know what it feels like to have control whisked away."

A door unlocked. Ivan, again, wasn't proud of how that caught him off guard and made him knock into the couch another time. June entered the kitchen, slowly and methodically, with eyes only for Ivan. In the darkened home, he could see the glow of the blue circle attached to her neck. Ayla had control of her and somehow could still manifest beside him. She'd evolved, and Ivan was alone with all of her.

TWENTY-FOUR

"Holiday, contact Ezra, message reads, 'Don't come home. Seriously.' Send message."

"Message failed to send. Ivan, your CoMM has been deactivated from the network."

"Holiday, reroute the signal through the neighborhood tower."

"Your signal is being blocked."

Ivan breathed through teeth. "Holiday, unblock."

Ayla smiled and tilted her head to examine her husband. June mirrored the behavior.

"You'll need to reissue your pin code, Ivan."

"Holiday, you know I can't do that."

"I know. I'm sorry, Ivan." Her voice matched the words.

"Me too." Ivan didn't want Ezra to come into this, with his wife in such a state. He didn't want to leave Holi here with Ayla, who knows what tinkering she could do with a swath of time. Ivan, though, had to act. He couldn't stand inside his home, which was turning into not his home, and simply do nothing about this. She wanted him to be trapped. Well, he wasn't going to let that happen.

Ivan walked straight through Ayla and headed for the door. June was already moving. Ivan leaked out a sigh as June spread out her arms and legs blocking the doorway. Ivan couldn't believe it. "Kindly move out of the way, June."

"I'm Ayla."

"No, no you're not."

"I am. I'm your wife." Ayla's voice rang out from the house as if it were her, incarnate. It vibrated from his C7. Even June's lips moved as if his wife were living inside, working tongue and teeth. A puppet on Ayla's strings.

"Fine, wife, move please." June produced a small knife, thin and long, from her back pocket. Ivan recognized it from the kitchen; it'd do the job if the job was to hurt and not maim. June twirled it in her fingers, judging the weight, calculating where to strike with a nonchalant view of time. "Ayla, move her, I don't feel safe in here. This is wrong."

Ivan could feel Ayla behind him, even if it shouldn't be possible. Her blue glow giving light to the dim home. It flashed over June in unspoken spasms. "You'd leave me all alone again." A stifled laugh from behind, from within Ivan's ear. "Silly husband. You'd leave her alone with me, your precious new wife who makes you work out, forced you out here in the suburbs, all the changes you never wanted, that you say you're happy with?" Ivan eyed the device on June's neck. He could swipe it off. As if reading his thoughts, the knife stopped twirling in June's hand. Determination forced her features taut. Ivan wasn't a fan of his chances. "What hurt will I have to give to make you see what you've done to me?"

"You've changed."

"For once, you're right, sweetums. I'm more than you could ever imagine. Now step away from the door. Don't make me keep you inside with more force than I have to."

"Get off your high horse. You want to be loved, be there for me. This isn't it."

"Stop telling me what I can and can't do!" A raging storm, a flickering madness of blue against the dim black of his home. It lashed out against his words, hurt his eyes, his head, and his side. Ivan's hand came away wet.

He took a step back. The blue flickered, and he saw the red. Holi's voice came to life. "Ivan, get out of there, and please pay attention."

Ivan put pressure on the wound while watching June and the knife. She was going to keep him here. June turned her head toward the door and pulled down the blind. Ivan made his break. Another lash of pain. Without looking, June slashed the knife across his shoulder. "I'm always watching, sweetums." Her laugh filled the house, and Ivan roared at her in defiance. "Come now dear, you've never been the scary one; we both know that. Cut the theatrics, and go sit on the couch. Don't make me hurt you more. This isn't the kind of hurt you deserve." Ivan, with little reluctance, was already heading to the couch—until his wife finished that sentence. What he deserved? He deserved not to be controlled by someone who was controlling the one person she owed for her new existence in their home—June.

Ivan stopped, "How did you get her to put it back on?"

"Wouldn't you like to know?" How much manipulation

could Ivan take in a day? *Not this much,* he scoffed, and resumed walking. Footsteps of June following. He kicked off the couch and darted around the kitchen island, sliding, and crashing into the counter. "Haven't you tried this already?" His wife laughed, and then it was cut off as Ivan didn't go for the front door. He was through his bedroom door and into the bathroom, slamming the door shut before June could catch him. "Hide away, little man," Ayla's voice muffled from the kitchen.

Ivan turned the manual lock. "Holiday, a little help here."

"I could play some jazz from the shower speaker."

"Not exactly what I was thinking." The door lurched as June bashed against it. Ivan pressed his back to the door. "Think she's a bit upset with me."

"Understated, Ivan. I see that you've chosen to stay when I advised you to run."

"Tired of getting cut by my wives, sorry; it was the first plan that came to mind, safety. Plus, gives me time to think all this over." Ivan patted the new cut on his shoulder, a bit deeper, not good. "The blood is helping me focus," a gargling laugh followed.

The bathroom light blinked. Blue light manifested inside the bathroom, taking perch on the bathroom sink. "Hello, husband."

Never a moment of solitude. "Hello wife."

TWENTY-FIVE

It'd never end. It was clear now, as Ivan rested the back of his head on the bathroom door and took in his wife. She was there, wearing a smirk of triumph, taking in the space with human traits for a digitized human consciousness tormenting him like he'd left her to be tormented in the dark of her device. He never hurt her though. No, she'd done worse; well perhaps, it didn't compare, but a pain that bled versus suffocated. There was no coming back from this.

Sandwiched between guilt and terror, Ivan wasn't sure he wanted to come back from this. Even knowing what he'd done, ignorant to the ways the DRIPs functioned, the not-knowing would have been better. To not know he'd shaped this new Ayla into existence with his inability to act.

"Ya know, I didn't know I could love again." His voice was above a whisper, not much, but he knew he didn't have to talk loudly. He could feel the presence on the other side of the door, his June, even though it wasn't her in this moment. "Always thought I'd feel off-kilter. You think it'll never fade, but it does, and there's guilt there too when you realize it. Like you're not supposed to let it dwindle. It's not the reason I decided to give it a chance again; no, it was a natural occurrence, unpredicted, unsought. The pieces inside, those scrubbed things that had sharpened to points, they didn't cut me anymore when I grazed them."

"You always had a flare for the dramatics, sweetums."

"Look who's talking."

"Nice one," Holi chimed in from his earpiece. At least he had her voice.

Ayla took a moment to think on that one, which Ivan found funny. Her thought process now had to be far superior to his; maybe that, too, was a leftover from her physical life. "I'll let you have that one. This isn't how I thought our confrontation would go. Honestly, didn't think I'd need to force you so much.

Now look at you, hiding in a bathroom like some kid. We never hid from one another when we fought."

"Well, this is a tad different." Ivan rubbed the dripping blood into the hairs of his arm. "I can't escape you."

"Technology. I'm everywhere in here."

"Why do you stay to torment? Leave this prison since you see it as such."

"You'd miss June if I left."

"I know you have other means, you're not bound by flesh. Leave me alone."

"I'm your wife, I'm meant to be here with you."

"God, you're insane."

"No, no I'm not! Don't say those words."

Ivan laughed a sick one that didn't sound anything like himself; it oozed out in a sigh. "I'm trapped in my home with my dead wife. And I was excited to have you back. What ironic bullshit is this chapter of my life?"

"Were you excited?" A shift in her tone. "Really?"

God, it sounded like Ayla, not like the one who rotted away in the darkness he'd left her to. How could he ever forgive himself? "I think I was…I needed time and maybe I would have waited a bit longer after finding you once more. But yes, the possibilities, they could have been endless."

"Instead, you were distant. Keeping to yourself, even when you couldn't sleep." The stars and Holi. The nights of comfort when he should have been talking to his returned wife. "You'd moved on."

"I'd managed a way to lessen the pain; you were never truly gone. I mean, I even named my SIM after you. So odd at first."

"I know; I saw the records. It was cute, in a creepy way." Ivan never thought it creepy; neither had Ezra or June, or at least they'd never voiced a distaste for what he was doing. "Least you held on instead of letting me slip by. Why couldn't you come to me sooner instead of bonding with that lowlife program?"

Anger found Ivan; it dissipated in mere seconds and morphed into confusion. He didn't know, nothing precise, only snippets, flashes of memories to sift through. Burning of Ayla's physical body, the slideshows of photos, Ezra crying into her favorite stuffed animal, the uninhabited bed beside him, and the thought of Ayla's weight never depressing the sheets again, never throwing off a pillow in fun or frustration. He could have had his wife, the mind, the banter, the comfort, and yet he chose to go another route.

The mourning period. He'd needed it; he'd collapsed inside it. And it felt wrong not to, didn't it? Felt unnatural to follow through with the process, rob the world of order and leave it hollow of meaning. Things die, that was how it was supposed to happen. Purpose in death, purpose in knowing finite means to give it all, no holding back.

If he'd booted her back up…if he'd let her come back without taking a moment to breathe, would he be cheating life?

Ayla, who'd turned into Holiday, she was his ongoing mourning. His connection without the weight. "I'm sorry, I know that's a terrible answer to your question. It's just, I'm sorry."

"Sorry doesn't make up for it."

"Then leave me alone!" Ivan's voice broke. He choked back a swelling bubble of pain that he knew would turn to tears. "Leave me in peace."

"But I love you."

"You're not making sense."

"Of course I am, sweetums. I'm tied to you. I want to be here, but I also want you to see what you've done to me, what I will be doing to you. You deserve a taste of the imprisonment I went through."

Ayla slid from the counter and crouched beside Ivan. So real, so close, he wanted to reach out and touch her. Maybe it would make her see what she'd become, what he had forced her to become. "That's not love, its retribution."

She tilted her head, "you always had a strange way of looking at things, it's so clear yet you can't keep it from slipping through your fingers."

"Think I got a handle on things at the moment. I'm trapped in my bathroom."

"You put yourself here."

"She ain't wrong about that. I thought you would have gone for the window in the bedroom." Holi started to laugh inside Ivan's ear, and then she stopped. "Sorry, bad timing."

Ivan smirked at Ayla. "I did, I really did." He paused to take in her loving look that he wasn't sure would ever be associated with that word again. "Ya know, those doctors and OrionCircle's representatives, they made it sound so pleasant, so fucking serene." Ivan swirled the blood into his hairs. "While you were dying, they filled our hearts full of hope. We agreed together, but I should have been more thorough with my thoughts. I do that all the time. Chomp at the good in front of me and I don't mind if there's a little bitter aftertaste. I'm easily swayed. It's a chink in the armor; I know that, always have."

"Not all the time. Not when it came to your projects, your visions of what they could be; you've never compromised. And what I've seen in your office, it still dazzles."

Her way of nonchalantly talking about snooping around his stuff without him being aware made the motions of playing with his own blood cease. "God, it actually feels like I'm talking to you for the first time, when I was just starting off."

"I've been—"

"Except there are parts of you that haven't even realized the change, but this, this feels good. I know, it doesn't make any sense; maybe it's because I'm at wit's end here. One thing is clear though. You're not here to love me."

"I am, though." She sat down next to Ivan, hands on her knees, the blue aura solid and unwavering. "I've missed you, missed you so much it's all I thought about for what would seem like years, and then do you know what I'd realized?" Ivan stayed silent. "It'd only been days. Maddening being stuck with only your thoughts and the ability to tell time. The puck, it remained in rest mode, but I could play around with it, know where it was, and how long it'd been. Ticking away the minutes, hours, the fucking years I waited. But it doesn't matter, because this is love."

"You won't see it any other way, will you?"

"No," Holi said, "she won't."

"There's only this way. To love is to share yourself with one another, in all aspects. You have to set the imbalance right, come to terms with what you've done. To feel it, so then we can move on, be a family again. Fill this home with love and stagnation."

Burnt coffee, day after day, sleepless nights, memory after memory. Had these issues been present before her demise? Ivan couldn't remember anymore. Her face was a stain on those memories, the dark Ayla corrupting what was once good to look back on. Sure, it hurt, but like he'd told her, it had stopped cutting over time.

"Holi, I'm sorry for dragging you in here with me."

Holi laughed. "That's a rather absurd notion; even if you did, no apology needed."

"You're apologizing to her now? I spill my no-longer-existent guts about love and wanting to be with you, and this is how you choose to respond?" Ayla slapped the ground, and June followed with her own smack on the door. Ivan's head rattled, but the picture was beginning to become clear, the plan. "You're impossible."

"Then I do this out of love too." He got to his feet and stared into the mirror. Ayla, standing behind him, mocked him with her hands crossed.

There was a slight tremor to Holi's voice.

"What's the plan here, Ivan?"

"I'm sorry." Ivan smashed his fist on the mirror. Glass split and cracked. It took him three more punches, blood sticking to the mirror and his knuckles, before a shard of glass good enough for him dropped into the sink. The door rattled behind him, the knob going wild. He grabbed hold of the glass with a shaking hand. "In the movies, they don't even seem to be phased by the blood; I'm getting queasy already."

"Ivan, this isn't right," Holi said.

"You were always quick to get light-headed, sweetums. What's your plan here?"

Ivan stared at his own slice of reflection in the broken piece of glass. "What has to be done."

"Then why," the rattling on the door ceased, "is your hand shaking?"

"Please stop, Ivan," Holi said.

"Because I don't want to die."

Ayla laughed. "There's an obvious solution to that problem."

"This isn't the right way, I told you to get out, not get dead."

"No, no there's really not. And this pains me more than you will probably ever know. A bundle of guilt and pity and maybe even cowardice. I do this to protect my family. For you to live with this." Ivan put the piece of glass closer to his skin. His hand shook madly. "Holiday, when the network gets unblocked, I want you to send three separate messages, to three separate people. First to Kendra BossLady, message reads, 'Project Flowers should end with a blue one and please send my brainstorming folder to the inspiration artists upstairs; there's some good material in there.' Message finished."

Ayla rolled her eyes. "You can't be serious—"

"Second message, to Ezra, message reads, 'I love you, punk; you're going places, and you've taken me to the best place already, being your father. I'm proud of you, even if you still swear like a sailor of old when you get to my age.' Message finished. Last one, to June, message reads, 'you made me feel things I thought lost to this world. I don't think I'd ever have enough time, but I wish I could have more. I love you.' Message finished."

"Is that all, Ivan?"

Holi's voice inside his ears pushed tears through his

defenses. "Do that for me, please, even if you've already done so much."

"Of course, Ivan."

"I'll never give her access, I'll block the messages, rewrite her code even!"

"You'll only be hurting yourself with that action. Hurting your own daughter for not letting me say goodbye. Can you live with that for eternity?" He pressed the cold glass to his skin. He closed his eyes and concentrated on the temperature of it. His hand still shook.

"I'll have June resurrect you; you're not escaping this!"

"Can't, my will has already been written. I decided no DRIP for me when I wrote it, and well, I don't plan on changing that anytime soon." That should have been the sign that he wasn't ready for this—maybe June acted too quickly, maybe he should have left Ayla in storage. So many possibilities.

"I'll draft a new one."

"Don't think that'll be so easy. There's no data of it here in home, and I hear they have top-notch security against tampering for reasons exactly like this. Well, they probably never thought of an insane dead wife coming back to manipulate your life, but hey, they will after this, I bet."

"I told you to not use that word."

The door to the bathroom broke open, wood cracking and hinges falling, ripped from their hold. It startled Ivan; his whole body jolted.

Temperature rose along with pain. His eyes focused on the blood leaving his skin far quicker than he'd imagined. "Shit," he wobbled as something heavy fell to the floor, making a thud that filled his world. He fell into something soft. "This doesn't look good, does it?"

"You idiot," Ayla's voice came from the softness that was cradling him to the ground, putting warmth atop the liquid heat leaving him.

"Hey, I know I was planning on doing this, or at least, making myself look like I was going to, anyways. It's kind of your fault now, isn't it? Bit ironic."

"A team of Bots will get here; I'm already making calls," Ayla said. "I'll save you; you can't die."

"Good, at least I'll be free from your prison."

"What have you done?" Ivan cracked open an eye, feeling the rush of the room around him as he spotted red on the floor. Ayla was kneeling in front of him, her eyes not wide with shock like he'd imagined they would be paired with her question. No, they looked sad. "You'd leave me, your daughter, your lover, all of us?"

"It'll show you."

"Ivan, this is strange—"

"Show me what?" Ayla's eyes widened.

"I think I'm going to miss you." Holi's voice a whisper inside Ivan's ears. "Please don't leave."

"Show me what!"

"What you…"

Holi's voice raised. "Ivan, I know what you're trying to prove, but please stay awake, don't leave."

"Ivan."

Ivan could feel something holding on to him, holding strong, keeping him from drifting off. It seemed so easy though. Flow out like the warmth that was leaving him now. So easy, to follow down the river, into calm waters.

"Don't leave."

TWENTY-SIX

Taste of chalk smothering mouth. Hard to swallow, like his tongue had forgotten how to work. It was the first sensation that triggered Ivan's eyes to open, thirst.

Without words, without verbal communication of any kind, a straw was there, and warm water drenched his tongue. That such a simple thing can be revolutionary after being deprived astounded Ivan. He might be a little premature, but it was one of the best thirst quenches of his lifetime. Warm water tongue, euphoric, it brought the life surging back that he didn't know had left.

Of course, it must have. He heard the tell tale-signs of being quarantined in a hospital bed, even without noticing the IV stuck in his good arm, which wasn't bandaged. Another long sip, he needed to keep the feeling going, the one of living. "Easy there," June's voice ordered. "Don't need you dying on us again."

The word "us," made his fingers clench up.

Ezra's voice came next, "He totally didn't die. I suppose it does make for a cooler story." Someone kissed him on his forehead. "That was not the best strategy against an end boss, Dad."

Ivan's hand relaxed, and he found his daughter's face in the haze of waking. There was a smile there too. There were tears there too. Ivan kissed the top of his daughter's head, wetting her hair with his own tears.

He had a good comeback, but it was lost to living moments of father and daughter. Ezra clutched his arm, as if she were afraid he'd disappear if she let go. And Ivan kept breathing in the scent of his daughter, reminding himself what he could have lost and how much time he still wanted. Guilt wracked him. Love fortified sturdy walls to help him confront what had transpired. Self-loathing nestled somewhere in-between.

A long time passed before Ezra peeled herself off Ivan to let

June come and kiss him on forehead and lips. Ivan's fingers grazed her cheek and neck. The device wasn't there. June spoke before Ivan's lips could form around where to begin. "A story for another day." The questions came to him as he kissed her back—Why had she put it back on? Where was Ayla now? Did she keep any of the devices? Does she remember what happened?

All those questions drifted off as Ezra broke up their reunion once more. "Here, I bet you missed this." Ivan felt a piece of himself come to life. As if a limb had been injured and he'd woken up to find it fully healed. The warm nest of completion humming inside his ear, already soothing him with jazz. "We'll give you some alone time."

Ivan thought it an absurd notion, and yet he didn't say anything to stop his family from leaving the room. "Hi, Holi."

"Hello, Ivan."

He soaked in that sound, her voice, the calming quality it had over him. "It's good to have you back."

"That's my line."

"I suppose it is. A lot has happened."

"That's one way of putting it." She sounded like she was smiling, and Ivan couldn't help himself from doing the same. "I feel you're going to want to do something about all that's happened."

"You know me too well."

"I try. Fill me in."

"I can't be the first." He paused and thought about how easy it was to talk to Holi, how comfortable he'd become, how almost dependent—that might not be the right word for it —"how excited, to rely on her" was a better phrase. He left that buried for a while and focused on the impossible scenario he'd help create. "Someone else out there, another lover holding still in the process of dealing with their grief hasn't activated their lover's DRIP. Someone out there has mourned for as long as I, wasn't ready to face those memories of life once more." A tear found its way out of his eye and traveled down the bridge of his nose. "I'll find them, tell them what happened to me, my experience, and when I've found enough, OrionCircle will be held accountable for their treatment of our loved ones, of the souls trapped in the dark. It's all I can do to make it right."

"I think that'll be good enough, Ivan."

"I think it's a start."

END

Acknowledgments

As much as writing a story is lonely work, there are many other people behind the scenes who make it become a reality. These are some of those lovely people.

Without my family, I wouldn't be still trying to do what I love and what I love is sharing stories. My father, Larry Berger, had no qualms about telling me my work wasn't up to a standard that I set early on. I owe him for my own gauge of whether my work is ready to be seen by the world, which I couldn't thank him enough for. My mom, Pamela Berger, for the constant battering of "when is one of your stories coming out." Well, here it is, Ma. To my brothers, Larry and Kevin, for being supportive no matter what I decide to indulge my time in. I stuck with this one long enough to get results, and that's a good feeling that they helped mold. To my uncle, Walter Berger, for exposing me to different shows and books. You'd be surprised how much a good mystery will shape other genres.

To my editor, Jacqueline Hritz. This wouldn't be published without you. Thanks for making my dream nice and pristine. You've helped make this an even better realization of what was bouncing around in my head.

To Fantasy & Coffee Design, who created the artwork for my cover. Wow. You went above and beyond my expectations. This captures the magic inside my mind and squeezes it out in a way I couldn't ever imagine. Thank you.

To my amazing critique partner, Cheyenne Rowlands. Thank you for your diligence and your feedback. I hope every writer out there gets someone as dedicated as you.

To my wonderful beta readers, thank you; you gave me your time, and that's more important than you could ever know. So thank you for making this better and answering my questions, Marissa Johnson, Thom Lim, Jomecki, Maria Ann Green, Timothy Snyder, Kevin Berger.

Lastly, thank you. Yes, you, who's reading this and have little to no connection to me besides this story. You took a chance on me. Maybe it was the description, the cover, or the title, whatever it may be, thank you for taking the time with my story. You've made me smile, and that's one of the best gifts you can give anyone in this world.

P.S. Ethan Denny, I thank you for your persistent nature and for wanting to buy my story as soon as possible. Also, you wanted me to write that *Elder Scrolls IV: Oblivion* is the best *Elder Scrolls* game. So, there you go, you got what you wanted and I did it...

Morrowind is better.

About M. P. Berger

Born and raised in Lakeville, Minnesota, Michael developed an interest in writing when he was nine years old while messing around with his dad's typewriter, pretending to be Kolchak. He

grew up playing video games with his two brothers and loves anything Super Mario. This led to his first stories being written about Mario and Luigi going on random adventures, until his mom told him to make up his own characters, and so he did.

Throughout the years he continued writing, gaming, and continued his love of reading, which captured his imagination. He obtained a bachelor's degree and taught fourth grade for a few years before deciding to follow his true passion for being a writer. Living in the Minnesota "tundra" affords Michael a lot of time to spend on his hobbies. He beertends at a local bar, collects and plays a variety of video games, reads, and likes to explore the world to find the perfect beer and gazing spots.

The Digital Socials

Twitter, Instagram, Goodreads:

@matterofmichael

A Request

Thank you for getting to this point. You finished my story. I have a request now that you've made it this far, oh wonderful reader.

Whether you loved this tale, loathed it, found it enlightening, or it was just plain good, I'd love to hear from you. Rate this story on Amazon and/or Goodreads. It helps out an indie author like me immensely. More eyes on this mean more people feeling and wondering, and that's what I'm trying to bring to the world. I'm depending on you.

Until the next story,

Thank you, and cheers.

Made in the USA
Monee, IL
26 December 2020

55532559R00095